A
Harlequin
Romance

OTHER
Harlequin Romances
by BETTY NEELS

1361—SISTER PETERS IN AMSTERDAM
1385—NURSE IN HOLLAND
1409—SURGEON FROM HOLLAND
1441—NURSE HARRIET GOES TO HOLLAND
1465—DAMSEL IN GREEN
1498—FATE IS REMARKABLE
1529—TULIPS FOR AUGUSTA
1569—TANGLED AUTUMN
1593—WISH WITH THE CANDLES
1625—VICTORY FOR VICTORIA
1641—THE FIFTH DAY OF CHRISTMAS
1666—SATURDAY'S CHILD
1689—CASSANDRA BY CHANCE
1705—THREE FOR A WEDDING
1737—WINTER OF CHANGE
1761—STARS THROUGH THE MIST
1777—ENCHANTING SAMANTHA
1801—UNCERTAIN SUMMER
1817—THE GEMEL RING
1841—THE MAGIC OF LIVING

CRUISE TO A WEDDING

by

BETTY NEELS

HARLEQUIN BOOKS

TORONTO
WINNIPEG

Original hard cover edition published in 1974
by Mills & Boon Limited.

© Betty Neels 1974

SBN 373-01857-6

Harlequin edition published March 1975

Printed in Canada

857

CHAPTER ONE

THEATRE was working late; it had been a quiet morning with a couple of straightforward cases, but the two o'clock list had started badly, when a perfectly simple appendix had turned out to be a diverticulitis; and even though the next three cases had gone smoothly, an emergency strangulated hernia, pushed in ruthlessly towards the end of the afternoon, had made nonsense of the list. With barely a ten-minute break for tea, Mr. Gore-Symes, the senior consultant at the Royal City Hospital, was already three hours behind time.

Loveday Pearce, Sister in charge of the main theatre, had disposed her staff as best she might, sending them off duty at last, although late, so that now, at almost eight o'clock in the evening, she was left with only her senior staff nurse, Peggy Cross, a second-year student nurse who didn't much care for theatre work, and was consequently not of much use, Bert the technician, and the admirable Mrs. Thripps, a nursing auxiliary who had worked so long in theatre that Loveday sometimes declared that in an emergency, she would be quite capable of scrubbing up and taking a case. She nodded to that good lady now as she slid forward to change the bowls, and Mrs. Thripps, understanding the nod, finished what she was doing and took herself off duty too. She was already very late and although Loveday knew that she would have stayed uncomplainingly as long as she was required, she had a husband and three children at home; it would have been unfair to have asked her to stay any longer – they would have to manage without her.

Mr. Gore-Symes, assisted by his registrar, Gordon Blair, was tidily putting together those portions of his patient's anatomy which had needed his skilled attention; he would be quickly finished now, there remained only the sigmoidoscopy, an examination which would take but a few minutes. Loveday raised a nicely shaped eyebrow at her staff nurse as a signal for her to start clearing away those instruments no longer needed, and nodded again at the student nurse, impatient to be gone. That left herself, Staff and Bert – she nodded to him too. He was a rather dour Scot, devoted to her, but with stern views as to just how much overtime he should do. He disappeared also, leaving the theatre looking empty. Loveday collected the rest of the instruments in a bowl, gave them to Staff, handed the registrar the stitch scissors, Mr. Gore-Symes his own particular needle holder and the needle he fancied, and allowed her thoughts to turn to supper: it had been a long, tiring afternoon and she was beginning to flag just a little.

Mr. Gore-Symes stood back presently, put the needle-holder on to the Mayo's table, said: 'Finish off, Gordon, will you?' and wandered off to shed his gown. As he went he said over his shoulder in a satisfied voice: 'One more, eh?'

The last patient was wheeled in ten minutes later, and Mr. Gore-Symes, perched on a stool, applied his trained eye to the sigmoidoscope. He was by nature a mild-tempered man, but now the language which passed his lips was anything but mild. Loveday. used to rude words of all kinds after four years as a Theatre Sister, raised her eyebrows briefly, accepted her superior's apology with calm, and thanked God silently that she had had the forethought to lay up a trolley against just such an unfortunate eventuality as this one.

'Another . . .' the surgeon bit back another word, 'diverticulitis, Loveday. How long will you need?'

'I'm ready when you are, sir.' She forced her voice to cheerfulness; if she was weary, how must he feel? He wasn't a young man any more. She whispered to the ever-watchful Staff to let the ward know, and with the calm of long training, handed Gordon the first of the sterile towels.

The operation went very well; it was a little before ten o'clock when the patient was wheeled away and the night runner, who had been sent to give a hand, was dispatched to make coffee for everyone. But Loveday wasted no time over hers; she gulped half of it down, excused herself and went back to theatre, to be joined within minutes by Peggy Cross. They knew their work well; with barely a word they cleared, scrubbed instruments, put them ready for the C.S.D. in the morning, wiped and washed, polished and tidied away until the theatre looked as pristine as Loveday's high standards demanded. Only then did she say:

'Lord, what a day, Peggy – thank heaven there's no list until eleven tomorrow.' She was pulling off her

7

gown as she spoke and then the cap and mask she hadn't bothered to take off earlier, to reveal a charming face despite its tiredness; big brown eyes thickly fringed with black lashes, a straight nose and a generously curved mouth above a determined chin. Her hair was very dark; a rich, deep brown – a shade untidy by now, but normally drawn back into a thick twist above her slender neck. She was a tall girl and not thin, but she had a graceful way of moving which made her seem slimmer than she was. She walked slowly across the theatre now, flung her discarded garments into the bin, rolled down her sleeves, and stood waiting for her staff nurse, a small, plump girl with a round cheerful face, which, even after several hours of overtime for which she wouldn't get paid, was still smiling.

'Supper?' she asked Loveday as they left the theatre together. Loveday shut the doors carefully behind her and paused at her office. 'Not for me, thanks – you go on. I'm going to do the books and make a pot of tea when I get over to the Home.' She yawned widely, added a good night, and sat down at her desk. The night sister who took theatre would be along presently; she would hand the keys over to her, in the meantime she could get the operation list finished.

She reached her room finally, tossed off her cap, crammed her feet into her slippers and prepared to go along to the pantry and make tea. Most of her friends were out, and for once she was glad to be on her own; bath and bed seemed very attractive.

She was half way to the door when it was flung open and a girl came in. She was a tall young woman, as tall as Loveday, but whereas Loveday was vividly dark, this girl was fair, with ash-blonde hair and bright blue eyes and generous curves. She stopped in the doorway and cried dramatically and with faint pettishness, 'Loveday – I thought you would never come! I have waited and waited. I am in the greatest trouble.'

Loveday saw that the tea kettle would have to wait. She started to take off her uniform instead; Rimada was her greatest friend and she liked her enormously, even while she was sometimes impatient of her inability to accept life as it came. Possibly this was because the Dutch girl was an only child, hopelessly spoilt by a doting mother and used to having her own way. When Loveday had first become friendly with her, she had asked why she had ever taken up nursing – and in a country other than her own, too – to be told that it had all been the doing of her guardian, a cousin older than herself, a man, Rimada had declared furiously, who delighted in making her do things she had no wish to do.

'Didn't you want to be a nurse, then?' Loveday had asked.

'Of course,' Rimada had insisted vehemently, 'but when I wished it, not he. There was a young man, you understand – he wanted to marry me and I thought it might be rather fun, but Adam would not allow it, so I told him that I would retire from the world and be a nurse, and he arranged it all so quickly that I had no time to change my mind.' She had turned indignant blue eyes upon Loveday, who had said roundly: 'Oh, Rimmy, what rubbish – no one can make people do

9

things they don't want to do, not these days.'

'Adam can,' Rimada had said simply, 'until I am twenty-five.'

Now Loveday eyed Rimada's stormy countenance as she got into her dressing gown. 'What's up?' she asked. 'Don't tell me that Big Bertha has been at you again?'

Big Bertha was the Senior Nursing Officer on the Surgical Block where Rimada was in charge of a women's surgical ward.

'Far worse,' breathed Rimada, 'it is Adam.'

Loveday took the pins out of her hair and allowed it to fall in a thick curtain down her back. 'Look,' she began, 'I've had a simply foul time since two o'clock – do you mind if we talk about it over a cup of tea?'

Rimada was instantly contrite. 'I am a selfish girl,' she declared in the tones of one who doesn't really believe what she is saying. 'We will make tea and I will myself go to the warden's office and request sandwiches.'

Loveday was making for the pantry. 'You do that,' she advised. 'You're the only one of us who can wheedle anything out of Old Mossy.' Which was indeed true; perhaps because Rimada had, for the whole of her life, expected – and had – her wishes fulfilled as soon as she uttered them, and Old Mossy had recognized the fact that to say no would have been a useless waste of time. Rimada, Loveday reflected as she spooned tea into the pot, had an arrogance of manner when she wanted her own way – not arrogance, she corrected herself, merely a certainty that no one would gainsay her.

She bore the tea-tray back to her room and found Rimada already there, the promised sandwiches on a plate and a packet of crisps besides.

'Wherever did you get those?' she demanded.

'I asked Old Mossy for them,' Rimada smiled in triumph. 'I can get anything I want,' she stated without conceit.' Her face clouded. 'Excepting when the horrible Adam does not wish it.'

Loveday drank tea and bit into a sandwich. There were a nice lot of them, all cheese, and the teapot was a large one. She relaxed, tucked her feet under her on the bed, added more sugar to her tea and said briefly: 'Tell.'

'I am in love with Terry,' began Rimada, a statement which drew forth no surprise on Loveday's part; Rimada fell in and out of love with almost monotonous frequency.

'That new houseman on Surgical? He's a head shorter than you are!'

Rimada frowned. 'That has nothing to do with it – I do not care in the least. He thinks of me as a Rhine Maiden.' She looked rapt.

Loveday looked astonished. 'A what? But you're Dutch – they were Germans, weren't they, with enormous bosoms and dreadfully warlike.' She studied her friend. 'He's got it all wrong,' she finished in a kindly way, and took another bite of her sandwich.

Rimada looked put out. 'It is a compliment.'

'What happened to Arthur?' asked Loveday. Arthur had been in evidence for some weeks; he worked in the

Path Lab, and while a young man of unassuming manner, had been more or less harmless.

'He wears glasses.'

Loveday nodded. 'Yes, I see what you mean.' She didn't much care for glasses herself, although several of the young gentlemen who had engaged her fancy from time to time had worn them. She poured more tea for them both. 'Well, even if this Terry's shorter than you are, I don't suppose it matters. You said something about your guardian – do they know each other or something?'

Rimada's eyes glinted with rage. 'No – how could they? But Terry wants to marry me, and this evening I telephoned Adam and told him that I wished it also. He laughed . . .' her voice shook with temper. 'He said that Terry sounded like a young idiot who was after my money and I could count on him never giving his consent.'

'You'll be twenty-five in a year's time,' Loveday reminded her. 'That's not long to wait, he can't stop you then.'

'I do not wish to wait,' stated Rimada heatedly. 'I wish to marry now, and so also does Terry.'

'But he doesn't earn enough to keep you,' Loveday pointed out.

'I know that, but we can live on my money. I have a great deal of it, you know.'

'But your guardian won't let you have it; you've just said so.' Loveday frowned. 'And I can't say that I altogether blame him, however dreary he is about it. You don't know much about Terry, do you? I mean, he's only been here about three weeks. I know you've been out with him, but that's not very . . .'

'Do not be an old maid,' begged her friend tartly.

'At twenty-seven you are perhaps getting . . .' She paused, at a loss for a word.

'Stuffy,' supplied Loveday cheerfully. 'I daresay I am.'

Rimada was instantly penitent. 'Oh, Loveday, I did not mean that! You are so pretty, and all the men like you and really you do not look as old as you are.' She smiled engagingly. 'But you do not love easily, do you? I do not know why – it is so easy a thing to do.'

'Oh, well, I daresay I'll meet a man I want to marry one day.'

'And if you do not?'

'I'll not marry. Now, let's get back to Terry. What's he got to say about all this?'

'He is most unhappy; he wished to marry me as soon as he could get a licence.'

'Then why doesn't he? You're twenty-one, you know.'

'But if I marry before I am twenty-five without Adam's consent, I do not have any money.'

Loveday stared at her friend. The conversation was getting repetitive. Terry might be in love, but he might be in love with money as well. The guardian, cagey old dragon though he might be, would naturally think that. 'I should wait a bit.' she counselled. 'Why not go over to Holland and talk to him?'

'Talk to Adam?' Rimada asked with something like horror. 'He supposes me to be a child; he laughs a little

13

and tells me to grow up and that I am foolish.' Her eyes narrowed. 'But perhaps, if I have an idea, dear Loveday, you will help me.'

'Not now, I won't – I'm dog tired.'

'Silly – not now, of course. But if I should have a very clever idea perhaps I could not carry it out without your help.'

'I am not making any promises.'

'It will be nothing bad, I promise you, but I want my own way and there must be something I can do to make Adam give in – if we were already married, how could he help it? We are a large family – everyone would be angry with him if he leaves me to live in poverty when I have so big a fortune.'

Loveday shook her head. 'No, I couldn't do that,' she protested. 'It wouldn't be cricket.'

'Cricket? But I do not wish to play cricket, I wish to get married.' Rimada looked put out. 'You English and your games!' she added irritably.

'Sorry, ducky.' Loveday got off the bed and stacked the tea-things on to the tray. 'I'd love to help you, but not to go behind your guardian's back. I still think that you – and Terry, why not? – should go to Holland and see him. He can't be that awful.' She paused as a thought struck her. 'Why not get at him through his wife?'

Rimada giggled. 'He has no wife, he is a gay bachelor.'

Loveday padded along to the pantry, Rimada behind her. The guardian, she imagined, was a Professor Higgins without the charm, and with a middle-

14

aged eye for the girls. 'Let's sleep on it,' she suggested. 'There must be something – some way of getting round him. And there's no hurry, is there? I mean, you've only known Terry for a few weeks, haven't you?'

'I shall love him for ever,' declared her friend dramatically. 'But I will have patience for a day or two while you think of something, dear Loveday; you are so clever.'

She smiled winningly, said good night and tripped away to her own room, to reappear a moment later. 'There is a hat in a little shop in Bond Street,' she rolled her fine eyes, 'it is so charming – it would do for my wedding – pale blue . . .'

'And wildly expensive, I'll be bound.'

Rimada shrugged. 'Oh, yes, but I want it.' She smiled with great charm. 'And I shall buy it tomorrow.' She disappeared once more, and Loveday, left alone, got ready for her bath while she pondered Rimada's wish to marry Terry Wilde. She felt sure that if she could persuade her to wait a week or two, she would either have fallen out of love, or realized that the only thing to do was to get her guardian on her side. Loveday, brushing her hair as she paced round her room, frowned in thought, she didn't like Terry very much – he was young and good-looking and had a charm of manner which somehow didn't ring true; there were quite a number of nurses in the hospital who found him attractive, but she thought that there was very little underneath the facile charm. He had worked in theatre once or twice and she hadn't been impressed; she had had the feeling that he wasn't very good at his job and hid the fact under a showy pretence of knowledge. She got into bed and turned out the light, quite resolved to have nothing to do with her friend's hare-brained schemes.

A resolve she was to break within a very short time – the next day in fact. The list had been short and had gone without a hitch; there was a heavy list for the afternoon, though, and the first operation was to be done by some specialist, Gordon had told her, apologizing at the same time for not having warned her earlier in the day, but Mr. Gore-Symes hadn't been perfectly certain that he was coming; it was some new technique this professor something-or-other had perfected, and the old man was deeply interested in it. 'I believe the fellow brings his own instruments,' he concluded.

'In that case,' Loveday had told him, 'he'd better hand them over pretty smartish, or we shall all be standing around waiting for them. Do the C.S.D. do them or am I supposed to see to it, I wonder? Why doesn't someone tell me?'

Gordon had grinned. 'Haven't the faintest, but I'm sure you'll cope.' He had gone off to his lunch, whistling cheerfully, and she, in her turn, had gone off to hers.

She had stayed longer than she had intended, sitting at table, sipping her post-prandial tea, deeply absorbed in the ever-interesting topic of clothes – so long, in fact, that she had no time to go to her room and do her hair and her face; not that it would matter a great deal, for she would be wearing a mask for the rest of the afternoon. She tore through the bleak Victorian corridors which would bring her to the lift taking her to the theatre block; the Royal City had been modernized on several separate occasions, various well-meaning persons taking it in turns to have an architect's finger in their Utopian pie, so that the whole place was a complexity of antiquated staircases, underground passages, gigantic pipes which made hollow noises in the dead of night, and hyper-modern lifts, automatic doors and a magnificent entrance hall, which had been designed to contain the very latest in communication panels, kiosks for visitors, a flower stall even, and which had never quite got to this stage, so that Parkinson, the head porter, still held its traffic in the hollow of his aged but iron hand.

The theatre block had been completed, however, and it was a splendid one, with Loveday in charge of it, aided by two junior Sisters, who ran the smaller theatres and relieved her when she went off duty. They got on well, the three of them; she was thinking about that as she skipped down a quite unnecessary flight of steps and began to run along the curved passage which ran round the back of the entrance hall. She was lucky, she considered, unlike poor Rimada, who disliked and was disliked by Big Bertha and was unable to laugh about it. She quickened her pace slightly and shot round the next bend, slap into the arms of someone coming in the opposite direction. A man, a very tall, very large man, no longer young but possessing the kind of good looks which would catch any female eye. Loveday just had time to see that for herself as he put

17

his hands on her shoulders to steady her and then held her away from him to take a good look. His eyes were blue, she noted with interest, and at the moment positively frosty. She smiled nicely, none the less, and said pleasantly: 'So sorry – I'm in a hurry.'

'My dear good girl,' he drawled in a deep voice and in what she considered to be a very ill-humoured tone, 'I find it surprising that a member of the hospital staff – a Sister, are you not? – should so far forget her dignity as to run, one might almost say, race on duty. You are on duty?'

Loveday eyed him with a slightly heightened colour and answered him with a decided snap. 'My dear good man,' and her voice was as cool as his, 'I don't know you from Adam, and what I'm doing can be none of your business!'

She twisted away from his hands as she spoke and continued on her way, her back expressing – she hoped – dignified disapproval, while she beat back a quite unworthy desire to turn round and have another look at him. She almost stopped when she heard his chuckle, but she was late already – besides, he had been very high-handed; a most unpleasant man, she told herself, safely in the lift at last, but undeniably good-looking.

Staff Nurse Cross, bless her, had everything ready, and she still had ten minutes in which to sort the special instruments which had been delivered to her office, get them into the autoclave, and scrub up. She was nicely settled behind her trolleys well before the surgeons' unhurried entry. Mr. Gore-Symes first, with his guest – her eyes widened at the sight of him; the man in the corridor, no less, behind. The blue eyes met hers with a blandly impersonal glance while Mr. Gore-Symes introduced him as Professor de mumble van mumble, from mumble. Loveday, none the wiser from her chief's indistinct remarks, inclined her head with hauteur and was affronted at the stranger's grunt.

'Loveday Pearce,' said Mr. Gore-Symes, quite distinctly for once. 'My Theatre Sister, you know. Runs the place very well.'

His companion raised thick fair eyebrows in what she could only describe to herself as an offensive manner, and turned to speak to Gordon before taking his place by the operating table. The three men arranged themselves without haste around the unconscious patient, covered on the flanks, as it were, by two housemen, looking apprehensive. Loveday waited until they had settled themselves before motioning her own team into place; Staff at her elbow, as always, the two student nurses well back from the table, ready to do anything she might require of them; Mrs. Thripps, on duty for the afternoon, standing back even further, her experienced eyes everywhere. And Bert in his corner, surrounded by the various electrical appliances which might be needed from time to time. She took a final look at them all, nodded her pretty head in satisfaction, and handed Gordon the first towel.

The operation was to be an adrenalectomy, and both kidneys were involved. As it proceeded Loveday felt bound to admit that this foreign surgeon was good; he worked fast and thoroughly, and not until he reached the stage where his own new technique was involved did he speak more than a few words. Even then she could not fault his manner; there was no hint of boasting; she was forced to admire his modest manner even while she recalled his quite unnecessary rudeness in the corridor.

It was a long business and tiring for all of them. All the same, it was with regret that she saw him leave the theatre. It was a pity, she decided, as she took off her gown and gloves and prepared to scrub for the second case, that she wouldn't see him again, let alone discover his name – even if she asked Mr. Gore-Symes at the end of the list, he would have forgotten it by then. She sighed and freshly scrubbed and gowned went to brood over the contents of her trolleys.

They finished just before six; the last two cases had been straightforward ones, and she had been able to send those nurses who were off duty out of the theatre punctually. She was off duty herself, but she was doing nothing with her evening, so that she sent the last of her staff away and, the theatre cleaned and readied once more, went to her office. Ten minutes would be long enough to write up the books, then she would take the keys along to Joyce, on duty in the E.N.T. theatre, and go off duty herself. Someone had made her a pot of tea, she discovered; it stood on a tray on her desk, with a plate of thin bread and butter on a saucer-covered plate. She smiled at the little attention, poured herself a cup and opened her books.

She had finished her writing and was polishing off the rest of the bread and butter when she heard the swing doors separating the theatre block from the hospital open and click shut. 'In here,' she called. 'I was just coming over with the keys.'

But it wasn't Joyce, it was Mr. Gore-Symes' visitor who entered, and at her surprised, 'Oh, hullo, it's you,' he inclined his head and put her firmly in her place with a cold good evening. She stared at him for several seconds, a little puzzled, and then spoke with relief. 'Oh, of course, you want your instruments. I gave them to Bert, but I daresay he couldn't find them – they'll be in the theatre.'

'Thank you, I have them already. You are a friend of Rimada's, are you not?'

He was leaning against the wall, staring at her in a disconcerting fashion. She said slowly: 'Yes,' while a sudden unwelcome thought trickled into the back of her mind. 'I didn't hear your name, sir.' She spoke hesitatingly.

'I didn't think you had, that is why I have come. back.' His voice was silky. 'De Wolff van Ozinga,' he added with a biting quietness. 'Adam.'

Rimada's name was de Wolff. Loveday said in a small voice. 'Oh, lord – I might have known, you're Rimada's guardian!'

'I am. I intend seeing her this evening. Is she behaving herself?'

She shot him a guarded look which he met with a bland stare. 'She always behaves herself, and I have no intention of answering any prying questions about her.'

He smiled lazily and she felt her dislike of him oozing away, to return at once as he continued: 'She has a remarkable habit of falling in love with every second

21

young man she meets. Who is it at the moment?'

Loveday looked at him crossly. 'Didn't you hear what I said? I'm not going to answer your questions. You should ask Rimada.'

He looked hatefully pleased with hinself. 'So there is someone – she meant what she said. The absurd girl telephoned me – besides, her mother showed me a letter. I suppose you are aiding and abetting her?'

Loveday lifted her chin. 'No. But now I've met you, I certainly shall!'

This spirited remark met with a laugh. 'By all means,' he agreed affably. 'If you are half as bird-witted as my cousin, you aren't likely to succeed, though.'

'I am not bird-witted!' She was feeling quite ill-tempered by now. 'Rimada's a dear, she can't help being – being . . .' She stopped, conscious of his amused eyes. 'She's afraid of you,' she flung at him.

He lifted his eyebrows and looked resigned. 'I can't think why; I'm kindness and consideration at all times towards her. Just as long as she does nothing foolish, of course.'

Loveday felt that she should really make an end to this absurd conversation; she wasn't getting anywhere with it, and nor, she fancied was the man before her. A pity, though; she would have liked to have got to know him better, even, as she hastily reminded herself, though she disliked him. She closed her books and stood up.

'Do finish your bread and butter,' he suggested politely.

'Thank you, no. I'm off duty.' She picked up the tea tray with an air of someone with not a minute to lose.

He took the tray from her and put it down again on the desk. 'Now from any other girl I might take that as an invitation. But from you, Miss Loveday Pearce, I think not. All the same, despite your cross face and your pert manners and your bad habit of running along hospital corridors, I find you a good deal more — er — interesting than Rimada.'

He leaned across the desk and kissed her on her half open, surprised mouth.

CHAPTER TWO

LOVEDAY stood very still. Her power of speech had left her; so for the moment had the power to think clearly. She was aware of a peculiar feeling deep inside her which she presently decided might be attributed to rage and a bitter dislike of her visitor, certainly she found that she was shaking with some strong emotion. Presently she picked up the tray and took it along to the tiny kitchen on the theatre corridor and tidied everything away in her usual methodical fashion before taking the keys over to E.N.T. and going off duty.

Once in the Home, she went straight to Rimada's room and found that young lady dressing to go out, an elaborate ritual which she interrupted to say dramatically: 'He is here – the horrid Adam. He waits below and I am forced to dine with him.' She tossed her head. 'I should have been spending the evening with Terry.'

Loveday sat down. 'Well, it's a good thing in a way. Rimmy, because now you can tell your guardian all about it. Why doesn't Terry go with you?'

Rimada applied mascara and leaned forward to survey her handiwork.

'Adam wished that, but Terry is suddenly called away – an emergency case in theatre . . .'

'Oh – I hadn't heard.'

24

'But you are off duty, so how could you? They will have told Joyce in E.N.T.'

Loveday reflected that she had left Joyce not ten minutes earlier and there had been no news of an emergency; indeed, there had been nothing in the Accident Room, and Nancy was very good at letting them know the moment anything likely came in, indeed, she often warned the theatre staff the moment she had news of an emergency from the ambulance crews. It sounded like an excuse on Terry's part, but perhaps it was best not to pursue that train of thought. Instead, she asked: 'How old is your guardian?'

'Thirty-six – no, seven. Almost middle-aged.'

Not middle-aged, Loveday decided silently; middle-aged men didn't kiss like that. 'I didn't know that he was a surgeon.'

Her friend swung round to stare at her. 'You have met him? How is that? Do you not find him quite terrible?'

Loveday skated round the question. 'He operated this afternoon. We bumped into each other when I was on the way back to theatre. He's super at his job, whatever else he is.'

Rimada shrugged her shoulders. 'Oh, yes; he is, how do you say? the tops. He is a Professor of Surgery, you know. He also likes pretty girls. You will take care, Loveday? He has charm . . .'

You can say that again, thought Loveday while she assured Rimada that she would indeed take care. 'Though as I'm not likely to meet him again, it doesn't matter, does it?' She felt a momentary regret about

25

that. 'I'm going down to supper – come along to my room when you get back and tell me how you got on.' She peered at her reflection over Rimada's shoulder. 'Gosh, I look a hag,' she remarked, and following her train of thought: 'I daresay your guardian won't be as difficult as you imagine – he's only human, after all.'

Her friend snorted. 'Bah!' she said through excellent teeth. The word carried a great deal of feeling.

Loveday had been in bed and asleep for quite some time when Rimada wakened her with an urgent shake. She was in tears, and Loveday, still in a half dreaming state, sat up slowly, forcing herself to wakefulness.

'Rimmy,' she uttered urgently, 'whatever is the matter? You're in floods!'

'Adam – I hate him! He does not listen when I say that I will marry Terry; he laughs and says that I don't know my own mind.' A fresh flow of tears choked her and Loveday, ever helpful, offered a handkerchief.

'He hasn't cut you off with a shilling, or anything drastic?' she wanted to know.

'Of course not,' sobbed Rimada. 'It is my money, is it not? When I asked him for some of my allowance so that I could buy that hat – you remember? – he gave it to me at once.'

She gave Loveday a rather hurt look because she giggled. 'Oh, it is funny to you, I daresay, but he thinks that he can bribe me, and I will not be bribed – I will have my own way.'

Rimada's rather weak chin set in stubborn lines. 'He is unkind, also he called you an interfering busybody and told me that I should run my own life. He said, too, that you are too clever by far and that bossy women are not his cup of tea.'

Loveday's bosom heaved with the fury of her feelings. 'He said that? I can well believe it,' she said in an icy voice. 'Anyone disputing his opinions or his plans would naturally prick his abominable ego.' She drew a trembling breath. 'You really want to marry Terry? O.K., Rimmy, so you shall; I'll help you all I can. We should be able to think of something between us.' Her dark eyes glinted, she was now very much awake. 'I'll show him what a busybody I am!' She smiled at the Dutch girl. 'I've got days off at the end of the week — change yours and come home with me, that will give us two days' peace and quiet in which to cook up something. Go to bed, Rimmy, and stop crying — you shall have your Terry. Good lord,' she exclaimed, suddenly furious, 'anyone would think it was the nineteenth century we're living in; he's nothing but a tyrant.' She added softly: 'It'll be rather fun.'

She didn't see Rimada until they shared a table with half a dozen other sisters at dinner time the following day, and it was apparent that the Dutch girl had quite recovered her spirits. For a moment Loveday wondered uneasily if Terry Wilde really was the best husband for her friend — a dear girl, but easily swayed and singularly bad at managing her own affairs, monetary or otherwise. But Rimada caught her eye even as she was thinking it, and smiled so happily that Loveday dismissed the idea as nonsense, and plunged into the lively discussion going on around her; Nancy Dawson from the Accident Room was getting married in December; she had just informed the table at large that they would be spending their honeymoon on a cruise. 'Madeira,' she breathed ecstatically, 'Lisbon – can you imagine? I can hardly wait!'

There was a general murmur of envy and interest and the inevitable topic of the right clothes was broached. It wasn't until they had left the dining-room and were hurrying back to their various wards that Loveday was struck by an idea so exquisite that she stood still in the middle of the passage to savour it. Supposing she and Rimada should go on a cruise? Quite openly, of course, in fact, they would tell everyone, including the hateful guardian. Even though he considered her to be a bossy busybody, he could hardly object to the pair of them going on holiday; indeed, he should be glad because it would take Rimada away from the Royal City and Terry. She smiled slowly; only he would be with them, of course, and once in Madeira – and Madeira would suit admirably because it was more than two days' cruising away, which gave them two days' start . . . they could marry. There must surely be such things as special licences there; Terry would have to find out. And once they were married, her guardian could do very little to change things; he would have to give in, settle Rimada's money on her and accept Terry Wilde into the family.

Loveday got into the lift, quite carried away with the cleverness of her reasoning. What was more, she decided as she pushed open the theatre doors, she would say very little to Rimada until they were on their way home; Rimmy, bless her, was no good at keeping a secret, but she would have her two days off in which to get used to the idea, and during that time she would have to be made to understand that discretion was all important – about Terry – she could tell as many people as she liked about the cruise. Loveday, greeting Staff with an absent-minded nod, made up her mind to go to a travel agency in the morning and collect all the brochures they had.

They drove down to Tenterden two evenings later, after their day's work. They went in Loveday's elderly Morris 1000, a car which, while hardly noted for its breathtaking speed and racy lines, maintained a steady forty miles an hour and seldom gave her any trouble. She would have liked something fast and eye-catching even though she was devoted to the Morris; it got her home with unfailing certainty and was, moreover, the result of two years' hard saving on her own part. Rimada laughed at it, and Loveday, understanding to someone who had never known any other car but a large Mercedes or a Porsche, the Morris was something of a joke, didn't mind in the least. Its steady speed gave her ample opportunity to talk, and that was what she wanted to do now.

Her plan was received rapturously. 'You are a genius,' declared her friend. 'I have thought and thought and I have been in despair.' And Loveday, used to Rimada's dramatic turn of speech, said re-assuringly:

'Well, now you can cheer up, it's all quite simple really. I've a pile of brochures with me, and there's a cruise to Madeira and the Med: in three weeks' time –

that will be the very end of September. You can book for the whole cruise and leave the ship at Madeira – with Terry, of course – I'll go on. at least, I haven't thought about that yet. You and Terry can stay there until you get married and then let your guardian know. It's the last cruise of the summer for this particular ship and the agency says it won't be heavily booked, so I daresay we'll get a cabin easily enough.'

'Clothes?' asked Rimada urgently.

'Well, I suppose we've both got enough to get by – I can't afford to buy anything much . . .'

They were nearly at Tenterden. 'We'll talk about that later,' she advised. 'We'll be home in a few minutes.'

Home was a nice old house on the outskirts of the pleasant little town. They went up the wide main street, lined with its trees and old-fashioned shops and houses, and turned off at the top of the hill into a narrow lane disappearing into the gentle Kentish countryside. The house stood on a curve, all by itself, a nice example of Elizabethan building, the last of the evening sunlight giving its tiled roof a glow and touching the garden around it with a splash of vivid colour. Loveday, who had a deep fondness for the old place, sighed with content as she caught sight of it, and just for a moment wished that she was spending her holiday at home instead of plotting against Rimada's guardian. She squashed this thought immediately, however. He deserved all he got and a lot more besides, and she would be delighted to prove to him just how right he had been when he had called her a meddlesome busybody; the words still rankled.

Her parents were waiting for them. Rimada had visited them several times and they considered her almost one of the family and once the first greetings were over, she was whirled away by Loveday's younger sister, Phyllis, a fourteen-year-old, home for the weekend from her boarding school nearby, and who considered the Dutch girl an authority on clothes, a subject very dear to her heart, leaving Loveday to have a brief chat with her mother before going into the garden with her father. He had retired as senior partner in a firm of solicitors in Maidstone and now he spent his days amongst his flowers, keeping the books of various local organizations in good order, and tinkering with his beloved vintage Humber motor car. They went to the potting shed and settled down for a gentle talk about seed catalogues, bulbs for the following spring and which roses he should order – he was good with roses, and Loveday, studying his thin good looks and a few extra lines which hadn't been in his face a year ago, entered wholeheartedly into the discussion because she knew how important these things were to him now that he didn't go to the office every day, and presently, in answer to his query as to when she was coming home for a week or two, she told him the vague plans she and Rimada had made for their cruise.

He was disappointed, she knew that, and her heart misgave her for a moment. 'I should have liked to have come home for a week or two,' she told him with regret, 'but I've another week in November, I'll come then. There'll be the roses to prune and plant out and those

31

fruit trees you want to replace and the hedges to cut – I shall be very useful.'

They both laughed as they started to walk back to the house.

Mrs. Pearce was rather more enthusiastic about the trip. Loveday worried her a little; rising twenty-eight and still not married, and heaven knew it wasn't for the lack of chances. Beryl, her twenty-two-year-old sister, had been married for six months, and her brother, the eldest of the family, intended marrying the following year now that he had a junior partnership in his father's firm, and Phyllis was still only a schoolgirl – if her darling eldest daughter didn't find someone soon she would be what Mrs. Pearce persisted in calling an old maid. She never spoke her fears out loud, of course, but Loveday, gently cross-questioned each time she went home, was well aware of them. Sometimes she shared them too; as her mother knew, she had had chances enough, and once or twice she had been on the point of saying yes, and each time something had made her hesitate even while common sense had told her that she was being foolish, waiting for someone she couldn't even picture in her mind.

They all studied the brochures that evening; it was going to cost quite a lot, Loveday calculated, but she would have enough if she were careful, but Rimada was quite positive that she hadn't nearly sufficient money.

'I am not good with money,' she explained to the Pearce family. 'I buy things . . .'

'Get your guardian to let you have some,' struck in

Loveday.

Rimada gave her a shocked look. 'I would never . . .' The look changed to one of delighted surprise. 'But I have thought of something – of course, I will ask Mama – she gives me anything I want.'

'Would you like to telephone her now?' asked Mr. Pearce helpfully.

She shook her head. 'Better than that, I will visit her. She will send money for me to travel to Holland and I will arrange that I have four days off together – next week, I think. I will ask her and she will be pleased to give me all the money I need.'

Her companions looked at her with interest. Rimada's faculty for getting her own way always interested them; they were moderately well off themselves, but it would never have entered Loveday's head to ask her parents to pay for a holiday she could well afford for herself provided she saved for it. Not that they weren't generous, but she was a grown woman, earning a sufficient income to keep her independent, and independence was vital to a girl on her own; especially, as Mrs. Pearce frequently thought, rather sadly, if she didn't intend to marry.

'If your mother has no objection, dear,' she murmured to Rimada, who looked surprised.

'How can she object? I am her only child and my happiness is most important to her. She will arrange a ticket for me to fly home and she will arrange that Loveday will come with me, and pay for her too.'

'No, thanks,' said Loveday quietly. 'I couldn't possibly get away – besides, even if I could, I can well afford the fare, Rimmy.'

But Rimada was persuasive; at the end of half an hour's argument Loveday had agreed to go with her; it would mean juggling with the off-duty, but that could be managed, she thought. But she insisted that she would pay her own fare to Holland and had to laugh when Rimada said plaintively: 'I find you so strange, Loveday, to spend your own money when there is someone else to pay for you.'

They went back to the hospital two days later, early in the morning, their plans crystallized by numerous telephone calls, a number of lengthy discussions as to the clothes they should take with them on the cruise, and a close study of the brochures. Moreover, Loveday had a cheque for twenty-five pounds in her purse which her father, in the privacy of the potting shed, had pressed upon her – to cover her fare to Holland, he had explained briefly. It only remained for them to book their flight to Schiphol for the end of the following week and reply suitably to Rimada's mother, who had arranged, after a lengthy telephone call, for her daughter to draw enough money for her flight from an old family friend in London, and at the same time she had said a few words to Loveday, making her welcome in a charming little speech.

Some days later, Loveday, packing a small case ready for their early morning flight, reflected that the time and trouble taken in adjusting theatre duties so that she could be free over the weekend had been well worth it; she was looking forward to seeing Rimada's home, and although her friend had assured her that

34

there was absolutely no chance of her meeting her guardian, she found herself, against her will, wishing that there was. Only, of course, so that she might let him see that his peculiar behaviour had made no impression upon her. He would have to find himself another pretty girl to kiss, she told herself crossly; as many pretty girls as he wanted, she added savagely, not liking the idea at all.

She had known that Rimada's home was a comfortable one, and she had supposed, without wasting too much thought about it, that her family were a good deal better off than her own; Rimada's remarks about her fortune she had always taken with a pinch of salt, for her friend was inclined to flights of fantasy, so she really was surprised when they were met at Schiphol by a chauffeur-driven Mercedes. No hired car, this, for the man was obviously a well trusted servant and friend, greeting Rimada with the respectful familiarity of someone who had known her for a long time.

'This is Jos,' said Rimada. 'He's been with us ever since I can remember. He doesn't speak English, but he's a wizard driver.'

They tore along the motorway in the direction of Den Haag; Rimada's home was to the north of that city, north too of Wassenaar, its fashionable suburb. As they went, she pointed out the more interesting aspects of the countryside through which they were passing and while Loveday obediently looked from left to right so as to miss nothing, she wondered if Rimada had been wise in her decision not to tell her mother the true purpose of her cruise. A decision which, she had assured Loveday, Terry had agreed with. If it were I marrying, thought Loveday, frowning thoughtfully at a windmill, I would have wanted Mother and Father to know – I would have wanted them to meet him too. But perhaps it wasn't quite the same in her friend's case. She settled back more comfortably and murmured her appreciation of a particularly fine church in the distance.

If she had been surprised at the car and the chauffeur, she was even more surprised at the sight of Rimada's home; a large villa, embellished with balconies, turrets and fancy brickwork, set in the midst of a garden so precise that it might have been ruled out with a set-square, and so perfectly kept that it appeared to have been embroidered upon the ground rather than growing in the earth. The massive mahogany and glass door was flung open by a tall angular woman, whose rather harsh features broke into a smile as they got out of the car. 'Jaantje,' introduced Rimada as they went inside, and hardly pausing, crossed the thickly carpeted floor to a half-open door.

The room they entered was lavishly furnished in a style to make Loveday blink, and in the middle of its superabundance of velvet curtains, brocade chairs, cushions, little tables loaded with silver photo frames, lamps and overstuffed chairs, sat Rimada's mother. It could be none other; here was Rimada, shorter and stouter and rather heavily made up, there were the blue eyes, as large as her daughter's, and the sweet smile. The lady got to her feet as they went in, the folds of her gossamer garment – quite unsuitable for the time of day – floating around her in an expensive cloud of haute couture chiffon.

'*Lieveling* – Rimtsje!' she enfolded her daughter lovingly and with some difficulty, because Rimada was a head taller and very much larger than her mother. 'And Loveday,' she turned to smile. 'I hear so much of you,' she went on in perfect English, 'you have been so kind to my little girl in her exile.'

Loveday shook hands and murmured; she had never thought of Rimada as being in exile before; perhaps her mother was given to embroider her conversation with the exaggerations which sometimes adorned her daughter's. And she had never thought of her friend as a little girl, either; her mother had undoubtedly never seen her offspring making a play for the numerous young men who took her fancy at the Royal City.

They all sat down, and coffee was brought in presently while they talked – Rimada did most of the talking, to such good effect that by the time they had finished their second cups and nibbled the biscuits which went with them, she had coaxed more than twice the amount she needed for her holiday from her mother; nor did that lady seem in the least surprised at the sum her daughter asked for.

'Dear child,' she said earnestly, 'it is quite ridiculous that Adam doesn't allow you more money. The least he could have done after forcing you to take up nursing in that dreary hospital, was to see that you had sufficient with which to enjoy yourself. I have mentioned it to him on many occasions, you know, but he is as steel; my motherly feelings have no effect upon him; he is a hard man.' She dabbed her eyes with a large chiffon handkerchief and went on with the same breath, 'tomorrow we will go to Den Haag; I saw a delightful little dress in Kuhne's, just right for you, dearest. A little expensive, I am afraid, but we must see what we can do.' She smiled kindly at Loveday. 'You like clothes, Loveday?'

The three ladies embarked happily upon this interesting subject and were only interrupted by the entrance of Jaantje, inquiring if the young ladies would like to tidy themselves before lunch, and if so, she would show Miss her room.

Loveday found her bedroom to be as elaborately furnished as the sitting-room; its comfort amounting to luxury. But not quite to her fancy, she decided as she walked round it, picking things up and putting them down again. It was a room to suit Rimada's mother down to the ground; Rimada too, she rather thought, but for her own taste it was a little too ornate and over-furnished. She found her way to the bathroom leading from it and eyed the gold-plated taps with something like awe; she had never quite believed Rimada when she had said that her mother was rich, but she could see now that she had been mistaken. She washed her face and hands, re-did her hair and face and went downstairs for lunch.

They went shopping the following morning. At least Rimada and her mother shopped while Loveday admired and tried not to envy. She considered Den Haag a lovely city and longed to explore, but it was obvious that there was to be none of that; Rimada, in the excitement of choosing a wardrobe of new clothes, had no thought for anything else; naturally enough. Loveday, with an eye to her slender purse, purchased one or two trifles for her family and refused to be coaxed or bullied, however gently, into buying anything for herself. It wasn't as if, she told her friend later, she was going to be the bride, and it really didn't matter a great deal what she wore as long as she was presentable. She had some nice clothes, perhaps not quite as new as she would have liked, but elegant and becoming; she had good taste and an eye for fashion and the fortunate attribute of wearing the right things at the right time. Later that day she sat on Rimada's bed, staring out on to the flat, tranquil countryside, swept by September rain and a bustling wind, and applauded suitably each time her friend opened a box to reveal some new garment.

'You're sure, aren't you, Rimmy?' she asked suddenly.

Her friend held up a blue crêpe dress. 'Well, of course. Look – it is exactly the colour of my eyes.'

'Silly – I mean about marrying Terry. It's easy enough for us to get a holiday and just go, but won't he find himself without a job?'

Rimada nodded, not giving her whole attention. 'I think so, but he does not mind that. He is far too clever for this job he has, you know. He will one day be a clever surgeon with an enormous practice.'

Loveday remembered his singular ineptitude in theatre and doubted it very much. All the same, he was qualified to a certain extent; he could always earn a living. Only, watching Rimada happily trying on her new clothes, Loveday wondered if that would be enough to content her. Just supposing her guardian didn't relent? How would she react to being the wife of a comparatively poor young doctor – and how could he hope to be anything else for quite a number of years to come? He would have to work for his fellowship to start with, and that would mean at least two years' hard study. She voiced her doubts: 'Supposing you can't get your money, Rimmy, do you suppose it would be better for you to wait a bit? You could be engaged, you know, until Terry has made his way ... if your guardian sees that he intends to make a success of surgery, he'll probably help.'

She watched Rimada's mouth set stubbornly. 'No. I wish to marry now, and so does Terry – nothing shall stop us.' She shot Loveday a speculative glance. 'If you back out now, I will still get what I want.' And Loveday believed her.

They went down to a rather splendid dinner presently, and friends came in afterwards. Loveday, introduced as Rimada's closest friend, was passed from group to group, thankfully surprised to find that everyone there could speak English. She was having a lovely time, she told herself firmly, hiding what she was distressed to find was boredom: if this was living it up with the rich, then she was disappointed. Sitting around drinking something she didn't much care about as well as not knowing exactly what it was; listening to chat about clothes, gossip about friends, little titbits of scandal about people she would never meet ... She had difficulty in not yawning, feeling mean and priggish for not enjoying herself more. Perhaps tomorrow, she decided, smilingly listening to a young man with long hair carrying on about the latest pop record, she would be able to go for a walk and see something of her surroundings.

She was getting ready for bed, much later, when the thought darted into her sleepy head that Adam de Wolff – she couldn't remember the rest of his outlandish name – wouldn't have enjoyed himself much either. She got into bed, dismissing the idea as being disloyal to Rimada and her mother, who were being so kind.

More friends came before lunch the next morning; Rimada's mother had an unending succession of them, it seemed. Pleasant, talkative people, who sympathized with her in their excellent English because she was a nurse, and in the case of the men, told her how pretty she was. Everyone was so kind and friendly, which made her feel meaner than ever at not enjoying their company more than she did. And Rimada's mother, kind though she was, began to irritate her, for she felt that the kindness was superficial and would disappear quickly enough if that lady's comfort was interfered with in any way. I must be getting old and crabby, though Loveday miserably; all this luxury and I'm not really enjoying it one bit – she might have liked it better if she had been brought up in it. She resolved to try harder; Rimada's mother was really rather sweet although she spoilt Rimmy beyond anything, and once or twice, when she had been crossed, the sweetness had cracked, and as for Rimada – well, she was a poppet really, with a heart of gold.

Rimada had a hairdresser's appointment after lunch and her mother always had a rest; it was easy enough to convince them that she would like to explore the country instead of looking at the shops in Den Haag, waiting for her friend. She started off briskly – there was wooded country close by and dunes in the distance. The weather was kinder with a blue sky and a hint of chill in the air. Loveday walked steadily looking around her as she went, stopping to study the farmhouses she passed and stare at the coated cows in the fields bordering the pleasant country road. The trees were further away than she had supposed; she reached them at last to find that they bordered the dunes, and urged on by a heady wind blowing in from the North Sea, she scrambled across them to stand on the beach at last and look at the wide expanse of water before her. It looked cold and grey, and already on the horizon the water was a rapidly darkening reflection of the great bank of clouds creeping over the sky. She stayed ten minutes or more and turned back regretfully, plodding over the dunes once more and then through the trees. The sun had lost its strength by now; she shivered a little in her jersey dress and walked faster. There was no one invited for that evening, she remembered with pleasure, and Rimada's mother had asked her to unpick and reset the stitches of some embroidery she was doing – she found herself looking forward to the quiet little task.

It had turned four o'clock by the time she got back

to the house. She went through the garden door, intending to slip upstairs and tidy herself; Rimada wouldn't be back for another hour, but her mother would be in the sitting-room. Loveday closed the door quietly behind her and then stood motionless in the hall. Her hostess was already in the sitting-room, having what sounded very like an attack of hysterics. Loveday started forward at a particularly loud wail and was brought up short by a man's voice. She recognized it immediately even though it spoke another language and registered anger. She was still standing, her mouth a little open with surprise, when the sitting-room door was flung open and Rimada's guardian, on the point of coming out, changed his mind at the sight of her, and leaned against the door instead, his hands in his pockets, a quite unpleasant expression upon his handsome face. He said: 'Hullo, Miss Loveday Pearce. Eavesdropping?'

Her mouth closed with a snap, her fine eyes sparkled with instant fire. 'I am doing nothing of the sort,' she protested in a voice throbbing with rage. 'How dare you speak to me like that? I've just this minute come into the house and you instantly abuse me!' Her bosom heaved on a deep breath. 'You're far, far worse than Rimada told me!'

He strolled across the hall to stand before her, effectively blocking her path. 'Surely you don't have to rely on her opinion?' His voice was silky. 'I fancy I didn't create too good an impression last time we met.'

She coloured faintly. 'You're insufferable! I . . .' She

43

was prevented from saying more by the appearance of Rimada's mother, her tears hastily dried, her voice nicely under control once more. 'Oh, you two have met,' she declared in a hostess voice. 'But let me introduce you, all the same. Loveday, this is my nephew, Professor Baron de Wolff van Ozinga – Adam, you know.'

She smiled coldly at him. 'And this, Adam, is Rimtsje's great friend, Loveday Pearce.' She ignored their stony faces and went on brightly: 'Just in time for tea, dear – we have been talking tiresome business and I am so relieved to have it all settled. Come into the sitting-room.'

'I'll just tidy myself, if I may.' Loveday ignored her hostess's obvious desire to have her company and went upstairs, where she took her time to do her hair and face while she wondered what the argument had been about. It had been a hot one, of that she was sure, probably about Rimmy. The quicker the poor girl got married and away from her guardian's bullying influence the better, thought Loveday, applying lipstick with care. Who was he to interfere, anyway? The head of the family, presumably – she remembered that he was a baron as well as a professor and wondered how she should address him. She was still trying to decide as she went downstairs and entered the sitting-room. After the sea air of the afternoon, she found it over-warm and heavily scented by the great vases of hothouse flowers on the tables; they must have cost a fortune – perhaps they had been the cause of the argument. She chose a chair as far away from the Baron as

44

possible, but he had risen to his feet as she went in and instead of sitting down again in the great armchair opposite his aunt, he walked across the room and took a chair close to her own.

'I had an idea that you might be here,' he told her affably. 'I hear that my feather-brained cousin is planning a cruising holiday in your company.' He saw her questioning look and went on smoothly: 'I had occasion to telephone her at the Royal City, and was told that she had come home for a couple of days.' He glanced across at his aunt, sitting on the edge of her chair, looking apprehensive. 'My aunt tells me that you plan to go shortly. It should be pleasant at this time of year.'

'I hope so,' Loveday spoke warily. 'I haven't been to Madeira before.'

His brows rose. 'Surely you will be visiting other points of call?'

She clasped her hands in her lap and stared at his chin – a very determined chin. 'Oh, yes – only Madeira comes first, you know. I believe the weather there is delightful at this time of year.' An inane remark, she knew, and he must share her opinion, judging by the glint in his eyes. But she had to say something; she stared down at her hands and failed to see the little smile tugging at the corners of his mouth.

'Oh, undoubtedly – a wonderful excuse for Rimada to buy a huge number of clothes.'

'The poor child never has enough,' put in her mother plaintively. 'You have no idea how important clothes are to a girl, Adam. It is all very well for you;

45

you indulge your every whim, I have no doubt, but you have no sympathy for your cousin . . .'

'My dear aunt, you wrong me. I have a great deal of sympathy for Rimada – as well as taking an interest in her well-being.'

He got up to hand round the tea cups and for a few minutes the conversation was safe and trivial, so that Loveday didn't need to think of every word she uttered. She had actually relaxed sufficiently to answer the Baron's civil questions about her work at the hospital, when the front door banged and a moment later Rimada came in. She stopped short in the doorway, the picture of consternation, as her cousin got to his feet once more.

'My dear Rimtsje,' his voice was suavely affectionate, 'how delightful to see you, and how charming you look – a new hair-style, is it not?' He crossed the room unhurriedly and kissed her on one suddenly pale cheek. 'I've surprised you?' he wanted to know gently.

'Your car wasn't outside,' stated Rimada uncertainly.

'Ah – nor was it. I took it round to the garage so that Jos could give it a quick clean.' He beamed at her. 'Loveday has just been telling me all about your trip – it sounds very interesting.'

Loveday, from behind his enormous back, frowned and nodded and made an urgent face and then smoothed it to instant calm as he turned to face her. 'We shall enjoy ourselves enormously,' she made haste to say with over-bright enthusiasm; Rimada seemed to have lost her tongue. 'The cruise lasts for two weeks, you know, and we're both keen to see Gibraltar and Lisbon – that's during the second week.'

She could almost hear Rimada's sigh of relief. 'There are some summer palaces,' she went on, glad that she had read up the guide books so thoroughly. 'We hope to see as many as possible, don't we, Rimmy?'

The Baron had sat down again, close to Loveday. Rimada cast her coat down on a chair and went to sit by her mother, who had remained silent but now broke into lighthearted chatter about mutual friends and various functions she hoped to go to. Her nephew waited for her to draw breath before he asked quietly: 'I hope you will invite me to dinner, Aunt.'

She was instantly in a fluster. 'Of course, Adam. Had I not already done so? I fully intended ... we have no guests for this evening, just we three women. You won't be bored?'

Loveday looked up and caught his eyes upon her in a thoughful stare. 'No,' said the Baron in the greatest good humour, 'I shan't be bored. On the contrary, Aunt.'

CHAPTER THREE

DINNER was unexpectedly pleasant; the Baron made no further reference to their holiday, but asked casual questions about their work and life in hospital, and presently he turned the talk to Loveday's home and family, neither of which subjects she wished to discuss with him. But Rimada, no doubt relieved at the safe turn the conversation had taken, answered his questions very readily, and launched into a quite unnecessarily detailed account of Loveday's parents, adding, for good measure, a meticulous description of her home.

'It sounds charming,' observed her cousin, and glanced at Loveday's expressionless face. 'You are interested in old houses, Miss Pearce?'

So it was to be Miss Pearce, was it? Her yes was cool, but not cool enough, or he must be a singularly unobservant man, for he went on suavely:

'Then you must visit my home. It is not perhaps as beautiful as an Elizabethan house might be, but it is an excellent example of eighteenth century Dutch architecture at its best.' He smiled at her with charm and her heart hurried a little. 'You are here for only four days, are you not? Then perhaps you would like to come tomorrow.'

Loveday hesitated: she wanted very much to see his house, and, she suspected, him, but she was going to refuse. An intention he forestalled smartly by enlisting the support of the other two ladies, who, to her surprise, instantly agreed with him. She found herself, without having uttered a word, committed to spending most of the following day in his company, and listened, fuming silently, while Rimada and her mother made arrangements with such enthusiasm that there was no need at all for her to open her mouth. Not that anyone would have listened to her if she had; the two of them seemed bent on arranging her day for her, and when she tried to catch Rimada's eye, she discovered that her gaze was being deliberately avoided.

Ten in the morning was decided upon as a suitable hour at which she was to be fetched; both ladies vying with each other to point out to her the advantages of leaving early – the weather, the beautiful morning light, the condition of the roads, the fact that Adam was spending the night, most conveniently with friends at Leiden, and could fetch her so easily. They gave her no chance to speak at all and now Rimada was looking at her in a most beseeching fashion; plainly, she was to be the sacrificial lamb on the altar of one of her friend's schemes. She glanced at the Baron, who had made no effort to coax her in any way, once he had delivered his invitation, and found him looking at her with the thoughtful stare which she was beginning to find disconcerting.

He left soon afterwards, taking a casually affectionate farewell of his relations and what Loveday considered to be a barely civil one of herself. The front door had scarcely closed behind him before Rimada burst into speech. 'You didn't mind, Loveday?' She waited until her mother had gone from the room. 'What a gift from heaven that Adam should have suggested that you should spend the day at his house!'

'Why?' asked Loveday baldly.

'You are so clever,' her friend replied promptly. 'You will not answer his questions when he asks them — besides, if he is busy showing you his house he will not have much time to ask them, will he? So I do not need to worry,' she finished complacently.

'Well,' declared Loveday, struck by this egotistical attitude, 'I must say I like that . . .' and was prevented from uttering the diatribe on her tongue by the return of the lady of the house, who echoed her daughter's views with great complacency, even though her reasons were not the same. 'Only fancy!' she declared indignantly. 'Adam believes you to be plotting some mischief — something to do with that young man, Terry someone or other, the one you thought you wanted to marry, *lieveling*, but I told him that it was all nonsense — a passing fancy, no more.' She smiled in satisfaction. 'I could see that he believed me. All the same, it is tiresome that he takes his guardianship so seriously — anyone would think that it is his own money which he minds with such care.' She sank back on one of the over-stuffed sofas. 'Not that it signifies, he is as rich as Croesus.' She glanced at the clock. 'I shall read for a short time, my dears, for I have had an exhausting day and I need to compose myself before I go to bed, so you may say good night now. I daresay I shall not sleep one wink.' She offered a beautifully tinted cheek to each in turn and opened *Elle*. 'Rimtsje, we will go shopping tomorrow – that green dress we were not certain about, I think it will do after all.' She nodded her head in a satisfied way and became at once absorbed in her magazine.

'I don't really want to go to your guardian's house,' declared Loveday as they went upstairs, 'and I can't think why he asked me.'

Rimada tucked a hand under her elbow. 'I can – you see, he may have believed Mama, but he wants to be quite sure about Terry. Don't tell him anything, will you?'

'No, I won't, but I don't think he'll ask.' Loveday spoke bracingly, although there was uncertainty in her mind.

But it seemed as though she would be proved right. The Baron arrived on the stroke of ten, driving a silver-grey Rolls-Royce Corniche, settled her in the seat beside him without more than half a dozen words, and those of a purely conventional nature, and drove out of the villa gates. He had barely glanced at her, and she, who had taken infinite pains with her appearance, was annoyed. She maintained a cold silence for several minutes, but as he showed no desire for conversation – indeed he might just as well have been on his own – she essayed a question.

'You live in Den Haag?' she asked politely, and then, remembering: 'I have no idea what to call you – do I say Professor or Baron?'

'Adam,' he suggested.

But for some reason she couldn't do that; she was

determined to dislike him as much as he appeared to dislike her, and one didn't call someone one didn't like by their christian name. 'I'll call you Baron,' she decided positively.

'No, you won't.' He sounded just as positive.

'Well then, I'll call you Professor de Wolff – the other bit doesn't matter, does it?' She was blissfully unaware that the Ozinga part of his name – the Friesian part – was as old as antiquity, well known and respected in Friesland, and he didn't choose to enlighten her. 'Call me anything you like, it will make no difference in the end,' he answered her cheerfully.

Of course it wouldn't; she was unlikely to meet him again once she went back to England. The thought gave her a fleeting sense of sadness. It would be a good thing when this day was over, she told herself; he was far too charming, even if she did dislike him. And he could at least carry on a conversation. She tried again. 'You haven't told me where you live.'

'In a small village called Akmarujp, near Sneek.'

Her knowledge of Holland was negligible. 'Sneek? Is that close by?'

They had joined the motorway and were tearing along it. 'Roughly a hundred and twenty miles. It's in Friesland.'

'But that's right in the north of Holland.' She was dumbfounded.

'It isn't in Holland at all – just as Scotland isn't in England.'

'Oh. It's a long way, though, just to show me your home.'

52

He slowed the car's rush and shot her a sidelong glance. 'Perhaps you would prefer not to make such a long journey.' His voice mocked her gently. 'We can easily turn back, I'm sure Rimada would love to have our company on yet another shopping expedition.'

She had a vision of Rimada's shocked face if that were to happen. 'No,' she said hastily, 'I – I didn't mean that; I didn't intend to be rude – I'm sorry . . . I should like to see your house.' And as she said it she knew that she really did mean it.

They stopped in Haarlem for coffee, at a charming restaurant in the woods, and the Baron, far from asking awkward questions, talked knowledgeably and in a manner to compel her interest about the countryside around them, and presently she forgot that she had made up her mind not to like him. They would go through Alkmaar and over the Afsluitdijk, he explained, and regaled her with stories about the Spanish Occupation, and when they reached the great sluices of the dyke, he explained exactly how they were built; the Rolls had eaten up the dyke's twenty-mile length before he had finished.

Once in Friesland, he took the road to Sneek and a little beyond that delightful town turned off on to a country road with glimpses of lakes on either side. The village, when they came to it, was small indeed, a red brick church, old and austerely simple, and a cosy group of small houses scattered around it, and half a mile further on, the Baron's house.

Loveday liked it immediately. It was red brick, like the church, square and two-storied and with no embellishments other than the elaborate plasterwork over its double door. It stood in a large garden, ringed with shrubs and trees and with wide lawns; she could imagine sitting there in the summer, or picking the roses from its great circular beds, still showing a brave autumn display. There were old-fashioned wrought-iron railings enclosing it from the neighbouring fields and a great gate, gold-tipped, standing open on to a straight gravelled drive to the door. Simple and large, and despite its simplicity, very homelike.

'I like it,' said Loveday as her companion helped her out of the car, and was rewarded by his smile. 'So do I,' said the Baron. 'Come inside.'

She felt instantly at home; not that it was in the least like her own home, nor for that matter did it bear the slightest resemblance to Rimada's home. Here were no fitted carpets, but a black and white tiled floor, plain white plaster walls with silver sconces set between a variety of paintings, and a high, delicately plastered ceiling, wreathed with fruit and flowers. The staircase was to one side, uncarpeted, with a wrought-iron balustrade and a brass rail, polished to perfection. She looked around her as they walked slowly across this pleasing apartment, and came to a sudden halt when the Baron bellowed 'Sieska!' and added something in an outlandish language as a woman came down the stairs to meet them. She was of middle height and stoutly built, with fair hair turning grey and a round, contented face.

'My housekeeper, Sieska,' introduced the Baron. 'She runs the house and me with it, her husband sees to the garden and her daughter comes each day to help her – a family concern, you see.'

Loveday shook hands, and said rather absurdly, 'How do you do?' and Sieska smiled widely at her. She smiled at the Baron too and said something which made him laugh softly as he took Loveday's arm. 'Over here,' he advised her, and as they crossed to an arched door: 'Sieska thinks that you are a beautiful girl.' He looked down at her, still laughing. 'Do you want me to say that, too?'

She looked up into his face, trying to read the expression in it, and quite unable to do so. 'No, I don't – thank you all the same.'

His eyes narrowed. 'Clever girl,' he murmured, and before she could query this strange remark, pushed the door open.

The room was the antithesis of his aunt's. Large and lofty, with french windows opposite a chimneypiece of vast proportions, its walls were white-painted wood, its panels separated by gilded beading. The floor was covered with tawny rugs, thin and silky to her feet, and the furniture was a charming blend of rosewood and satinwood and mahogany, the chairs and sofas covered in browns and oatmeal and amber with here and there a splash of unexpected peacock blue. The curtains were of the same rich blue, fringed and swathed in the style of a bygone period. Loveday's eyes darted from a table in the Greek style, circa 1830, to a bow-fronted wall cabinet housing treasures of porcelain and silver, and back to a satinwood side table with a marble top; they came to rest finally on a large golden retriever dog, who had got to his feet and was ambling towards them. There was a cat too, an ordinary tabby, curled up before the log fire. She turned a surprised face to her host and he asked instantly. 'You are surprised, perhaps?'

'No – no, not the room, it's exactly . . . that is, it's beautiful, just as I imagined . . .' She stopped, aware that his eyes were upon her, appreciative of the muddle she was getting into. 'The animals,' she explained hastily. 'I would have expected a Siamese and an Afghan hound at the very least.'

He mocked her gently. 'Then I have let you down sadly, I'm afraid. Meet Digger, ten years old and my devoted friend, and Moggy, who adopted us several years ago. Digger would have come to meet us, but he's strained a tendon and has to take things easily for a while.'

She stroked the hard round head and gently pulled a silky ear before Digger, with a polite swish of his tail, went back to his master's side. The door opened then and Sieska came in with a tray of drinks and the Baron said: 'If you would like to go with Sieksa, she will show you where you can do your face and tidy your hair and so on . . . come back here when you're ready, and we'll have a drink before lunch.'

Loveday followed the housekeeper upstairs, thinking about the Baron; he wasn't only charming, he was nice too. She damped down a growing interest in him as they went past a succession of closed doors, until finally one was opened and she found herself in a small room, pink and white and dainty, where she looked immediately into the looking glass with some anxiety, for had not her host recommended her to do her face and hair? – Perhaps there was a smudge or a spot, even. Her reflection looked back at her, as fresh as paint and needing nothing done to it at all, although, to be on the safe side, she powdered her small straight nose and made sure her mascara was intact; she did her hair again too, quite unnecessarily because she was suddenly shy of meeting the Baron again, but she couldn't stay there for ever; presently she went downstairs and into the sitting-room, where she sat down composedly, drank her sherry and made small talk, suddenly and strangely at ease again once she was in his company again.

The small talk lasted throughout lunch, eaten in a large, square room on the other side of the hall. It was furnished with an oval table and delicate Hepplewhite shield-back chairs and a sideboard with painted panels, and like the sitting-room, was full of muted colour. And the meal matched the room, simple, yet quite perfect and as a concession to her presence, she was offered an elaborate trifle which her host waved aside in favour of the cheese. Loveday, who loved trifle, had two helpings.

It was later, after they had had their coffee and she had accepted his offer to take her on a tour of the house that she realized that the conversation had taken a different turn; between his remarks about the various rooms they inspected, there were questions, quietly put, and leading, she had the wit to see, to the intended holiday. She answered noncommittally to begin with, but after a time, when he had given her a more than

57

sketchy history of a particularly interesting pair of *cassolettes* in one of the bedrooms, she turned to face him.

'If you want to ask me questions about us going on the cruise, I wish you would do so; I should like to enjoy looking at your house without being cross-examined by every chair and picture.'

He roared with laughter. 'Oh, clever Miss Pearce,' he murmured blandly, 'and what makes you think that I should be interested in your holidays?'

'Not mine, Rimada's,' she corrected him with asperity, and picked up a delicate porcelain figure so that she might admire it more closely.

'Just so, dear girl. May I have your undivided attention?' He took the valuable trifle from her and put it down carefully. 'Certainly I brought you here today so that I might discover what lies behind Rimada's sudden urge to travel, especially as only a very short time ago she was begging my consent to her marriage with some young man at the Royal City – he is still there, I take it?' He gave her a sharp look. 'Has she quarrelled with him?'

'I don't know,' said Loveday, truthfully enough, and was incensed when he replied, 'No, naturally you wouldn't, would you?' He picked up the figurine he had just put down and balanced it on the palm of a large, well-kept hand. 'You're not on my side, are you?' he queried softly. 'A pity. My fault, I started off on the wrong foot.'

'Yes, you did.' The starchiness of her voice concealed the unexpected pleasure she had in remembering the occasion. The starch had no effect upon her companion, however. 'Presumably,' he went on in hatefully conversational tones, 'men do kiss you from time to time?'

'Naturally.' She kept her voice cool and wished she had something to do with her hands.

'I am glad that we agree about something,' he said, and kissed her with a swift expertise which took her breath. Before she could open her indignant mouth to voice the tumbling thoughts in her head, he went on smoothly: 'You were asking about these *cassolettes*; used for perfume, as I'm sure you know. I believe they were by Matthew Boulton, and Craft did the enamel covers. I find them hideous.'

'I must agree,' said Loveday, her voice high with her efforts to control it. 'I much prefer the figurine you are holding.'

His mouth twitched into a smile. 'And so do I – but then I like girls, and she's rather lovely, isn't she?'

She turned her back on him and stared at the wide canopied bed with its brocade hangings and slender posts, then turned round again, because there was really nothing she could think of to say about it – besides, she suspected that if she did, the Baron would probably take the opportunity of being humorous about it.

He put down the figurine once again and said suavely: 'Wise girl – you never know what I might say, do you? Such an obvious chance for innuendoes, is it not? Only when you know me better, you will discover that I never do the obvious thing.' He grinned suddenly.

'Let us examine these wall sconces – silver, William and Mary, and quite a safe topic, shouldn't you think?'

Loveday wanted to laugh, quite overcome by the knowledge that if she had been allowed by circumstance to do so, she would have liked her companion very much indeed. The laugh bubbled up and she didn't attempt to stop it.

'You know, I was afraid you were never going to do that,' he observed pleasantly. 'We may be on opposite sides of the camp, but I can see no reason why we shouldn't share a sense of humour from time to time. I am not a monster, you know, only Rimada's guardian, for my sins.'

She just stopped herself in time from feeling sorry for him, instead she said in a more friendly voice: 'You have a lovely house, Professor de Wolff. Is your practice here too?'

He accepted her lead at once. 'If you mean, do I look after the village – yes, but I go to Groningen to my consulting rooms and the hospital, and once a week I go to Utrecht, and occasionally to Leiden, and to London from time to time.'

Her eyes widened. 'So you're not here a great deal?'

They had strolled out of the room and into a long, narrow corridor.

'Indeed I am. Unless I'm kept by some emergency case or something similarly urgent, I come home each evening. I am,' he went on deliberately, 'a confirmed bachelor – I enjoy peace and quiet.'

'Oh!' She was nonplussed; he had painted a monklike existence which hardly tallied with Rimada's description of him. She raised her lovely eyes to his and because she suddenly wanted to know all about him, asked: 'And would you not find peace and quiet with a wife?'

The grey eyes returned her look steadily. 'Certainly, but until then . . . You must not imagine that I lead a hermit's life, Loveday. I have many friends; they visit me here, I go out a good deal.'

She wasn't sure what he was telling her. 'Yes, well, I expect you do,' and then before she could stop herself, 'But that's not peace and quiet,' she pointed out.

'So I have given you something to think about?' He sounded satisfied as he opened yet another door. 'Now this room used to be mine when I was a small boy.' He ushered her into an austerely furnished apartment and launched into a detailed description of its contents which didn't allow of her getting in a word edgeways. He was still talking, smoothly and without pause, as they strolled round the garden, suiting their steps to Digger's stiff, slow gait. It was larger than she had at first thought, and at the back of the house, nicely screened from the house by a box hedge, was a kitchen garden of sizeable proportions. With her father in mind, Loveday asked sensible questions about sprouts, cabbages and potatoes, all of which her companion answered with commendable patience and an expressionless face; he even supplied a wealth of information about the rose beds, of which there were a great number.

'Father would like to see these,' declared Loveday.

'He's a great gardener, you know; I help him sometimes, but I forget the names of things.' Her companion murmured encouragingly and almost unknowingly, led on by his casual questions, she told him about her home and her family, quite forgetful of how vexed she had been with Rimada for having done the very same thing.

They went inside presently and had tea while the Baron entertained her with the histories of the various members of his family, long since dead, whose likenesses gazed down at them from the walls, and never once did he mention Rimada, nor, as he drove her back to his aunt's house, did he have anything further to say about their holiday. Loveday, after a little cautious conversational skirmishing, relaxed and allowed herself to enjoy her companion's company while at the same time reminding herself, rather half-heartedly, that she still disliked him, but long before they had arrived at their destination she forgot about that; probably he would annoy her with his arrogant ways and stern attitude towards his cousin, but for the time being at least she was enjoying herself more than she had done for some time.

They arrived at the house the best of friends; it was sheer misfortune that Rimada and her mother should be in the sitting-room, surrounded by boxes and tissue paper and with the results of their shopping spread out around them. The Baron took one look as he greeted them and observed nastily:

'There will be no good in applying to me to foot these bills, because I have no intention of doing so.' He stared round him. 'Anyone would think,' he went on silkily, 'that my cousin was contemplating a honeymoon rather than a fortnight's cruise.'

Rimada looked so terrified that Loveday felt impelled to come to her rescue, an impulse heightened by her hostess's weak-minded burst of tears. 'How very unreasonable,' she pointed out. 'Everyone knows that one needs any amount of clothes on board ship.'

'Ah – just so. And have you bought your outfit yet, Miss Pearce?' His voice was very gentle, but it was useless to suppose that he didn't require an answer. 'I have plenty of clothes,' she assured him, and pinkened indignantly under the leisurely study he made of her good but by no means new tweed suit. She remembered uneasily that she had been wearing it when she had arrived, and the jersey dress she had worn for dinner the evening before wasn't new either.

'I perceive that you travel light,' he murmured, 'something Rimada has never learnt to do. She has never learned the art of wearing the right clothes at the right time, thereby saving herself the infinite trouble of packing too many clothes when she goes anywhere.' He smiled thinly at his cousin. 'By the time you have paid for these, your allowance for the quarter will be negligible, my dear,' he informed her, 'but you have doubtless bought enough to last you for a very long time, and you won't need much money on board ship – I'm sure that Loveday will keep a careful eye on your purse for you.' He tossed an armful of dresses on to a table and sat down. 'For how long is this cruise? I'm so forgetful.'

Loveday frowned; he wasn't forgetful at all, only suspicious, and if Rimada didn't pull herself together and stop looking so guilty, they might just as well call the whole thing off. 'Fourteen days,' she told him, adding snappishly: 'We go from Southampton to Madeira, then to Tangier, Gibraltar, Cadiz and Lisbon, and then back to Southampton.'

'Delightful,' murmured the Baron, quite unmoved by her crossness. 'Doubtless you will make a number of friends on board, two such young and pretty girls.' He sounded like a benevolent uncle. 'You are young, Miss Pearce?'

She choked. Her voice, when she answered him, was a little too loud and held the faintest of wobbles. 'I am old enough to appreciate good manners, Professor de Wolff!'

He steeled back in his chair, impervious to belligerence, prepared to go on talking for as long as it pleased him. 'Exactly the sort of answer I might have expected from you, dear girl,' He put his splendid head on one side and studied her. 'Twenty-five – six?' he essayed. 'A little older than Rimada, I imagine, but only a little.' He smiled faintly. 'But perhaps you prefer to keep your age a secret? Some women do, I believe, once they have reached thirty or thereabouts.'

'I am not thirty,' said Loveday sharply, 'I'm twenty-seven, almost twenty-eight, since you're so curious.' She bit her lip at his slow smile and gave him a defiant stare. He got to his feet without haste.

'Not curious, dear Miss Pearce, I like to be sure of my facts. Well, I must be going.' He crossed the room and kissed his aunt's still wet cheek. 'I shall be seeing you again shortly,' he advised her, and smiled a little at her halfhearted response to this. Rimada replied timidly to his good wishes for a pleasant holiday, it was left to Loveday to look him in the eye and give him a firm handshake while she thanked him for her pleasant day. It was a nice little speech, completely wasted upon him, though, for he grinned down at her, her hand still in his, and remarked: 'How very polite you sound. I should so much rather hear exactly what you think, you know. Enjoy your holiday.'

No good-bye, no vague wish to see her again, however insincere; Loveday heard his firm footsteps, muffled by carpet, cross the hall. She was unlikely to meet him again – the thought gave her no satisfaction at all.

CHAPTER FOUR

THERE was little opportunity to talk to Rimada that evening. Only as they were on the way down to dinner, could Loveday ask: 'But why are you afraid of your guardian? You looked as though he was going to gobble you up – even your mother . . .' she paused. 'Is it because he's got a title?'

Rimada giggled. 'No, of course not, silly – how absurd that would be! We all have titles, you know – Mother is Freule and so am I.' She saw Loveday's puzzled frown. 'But it is too complicated to explain now.'

'Then why?' asked Loveday again with dogged persistence. 'He's not unkin.. – well, not really.' She looked around her at the luxury of her surroundings. 'And you seem to have just everything you could want.'

Rimada shrugged. 'Perhaps; Mama likes to buy things and so do I – we never worry about money – why should we? There is so much. My father left a great deal of it, you know, but Adam is always telling us that we are extravagant and that we waste it on useless things.' She smiled suddenly and looked like a mischievous child. 'How angry he would be if he knew how much money Mama has given me for our holiday; much, much more than I need. But half of it is for Terry, although she doesn't know that, of course.'

They had reached the hall by now and were standing in the middle of its flower-scented warmth.

'Terry?' Loveday's voice was shocked.

'Of course. I told him that I would pay his fare.'

'Rimmy, you can't – even if you were married to him he would hate to take money from you; he surely won't let you.'

Rimada tossed her blonde head. 'You are silly, Loveday – of course he lets me; he knows that I am rich.'

For a moment Loveday felt herself to be in strong sympathy with Rimada's guardian, however tiresome he was. 'Look, Rimmy,' she said urgently, 'even if Terry knows you can afford to pay for him, he will hate to take money . . .'

Rimada's mouth set obstinately. 'He does not hate it at all; I have given him money, three, four times.' She added coldly, 'We will not speak of it, for it is my own private business.'

Loveday accepted the snub with outward meekness, feeling a strong urge to find her way to the Baron at all costs and urge him to do something, anything, before Rimada had her own stubborn way. But he was a hundred miles or more away; even if she telephoned he would never believe her; had he not said that they were in opposite camps? And how could she tell tales on a friend? Perhaps, she thought hopefully, she might be able to persuade Rimada to put her wedding off for a little while, long enough for her to be quite sure. She seemed sure enough now, though Loveday still nurtured grave doubts about the bridegroom. 'Rimmy,' she began persuasively, and was urgently shushed because Freule de Wolff was tripping downstairs to join them.

The two girls were on their way to bed before Loveday had another chance to broach the subject. 'Look, Rimmy,' she coaxed, 'I've helped you a great deal and I'll go on helping you because I said I would, but I think you should tell your mother all about it before we go. Telephone her just before we go on board; it will be too late for anyone to come after us by then, so it'll be quite safe. Once you're married you can go home with Terry if you wish, and all the tiresome explanations will have been made.'

Rimada liked the idea. 'You think that I should do that?'

'Well, yes – your mother, you know – it would be only fair.'

'Supposing she were to tell Adam?'

'Not if you ask her not to. Anyway, he doesn't come as often as all that, does he? They may not meet for ages – long after you're married.'

Rimada nodded. 'I believe that you are right. I will do that.' She looked at Loveday. 'And you will be happier if I do?'

'Much.'

They went back to the Royal City the next day, back to the bustling, absorbing life within its walls. Loveday, plunged into the ordered rush of the theatre, had no thoughts to spare for anything much save her work, and when she got off duty that evening it was to find a note from Rimada to say that she had gone out with Terry – a pattern of ever-recurring frequency during the days which followed, and a good thing too, Loveday considered; the more the two of them were together the better. Marriage, she firmly believed, stood a better chance if the parties concerned had had a reasonable time in which to get to know each other. She was inclined to scoff at the various tales she had heard of love at first sight. There was no such thing, she reminded herself with undue vehemence.

The last details of the cruise were worked out; the tickets collected, clothes decided upon, rejected, and then decided upon once more, and the two girls went down to Tenterden once more, where they were welcomed with open arms, fed hugely, and given a great deal of advice by Mrs. Pearce. 'And you will be sure and send a letter from your first port of call – Madeira, isn't it? – or I shall be worried.' She looked kindly at Rimada. 'Does your mother worry, too, dear?'

'Of course, Mrs. Pearce, and because I am her only child, it is much worse for her.'

A reasoning Mrs. Pearce couldn't subscribe to but was too nice to argue about. She had four children of her own, and therefore, she reasoned silently, four times the anxieties which a mother of one might experience.

'You have enough money?' she enquired of Loveday.

She was instantly reassured by her daughter: more than enough, and if she was going to continue the cruise on her own, she thought silently, she would need even less than she had with her: it might be a little lonely, but . . . She cheered herself up with the thought that one was supposed to make a great many friends on board ship.

Back at hospital and two evenings later, just as she was about to go off duty, Gordon Blair flung open the swing doors as she was approaching them and ushered in Professor de Wolff. She stopped dead in her tracks, her only thought, and that muddled, that Rimada had gone out with Terry.

The Baron sauntered towards her, immaculate as usual and very much at his ease, his face wearing a bland smile. 'Miss Loveday Pearce!' he exclaimed. 'How delightful to see you again, although I must say that at the moment you appear to be suffering some form of shock.'

Loveday opened her mouth; something should be said, something polite, something to dull the suspicion she felt was hiding behind that placid smile. No sound came. She glanced at Gordon, rather in the manner of a drowning man grasping at a rope, but he didn't help at all.

'I say, you do look a wreck, Loveday,' was all he said, with all the candour of an old friend. 'Seen a ghost or something? Working too hard, I dare say. You ought to give yourself an evening out – relax.'

Relax! thought Loveday hollowly; how could she relax when she needed all her wits about her?

'A shrewd piece of advice,' observed the Baron admiringly. 'Don't let me keep you, Blair – much obliged for your assistance.'

Loveday watched with resigned despair as Gordon wandered off, shutting the doors with a clang behind him, leaving her alone with this man, who any minute now was going to inquire for Rimada. She would have to cook up some tale, and she was a bad liar, but she wasn't a girl to wait for the worst to happen.

'Good evening,' she began inanely, and managed a smile. 'Have you come to take Rimada out? What a pity you didn't let her know sooner. They've gone to supper and then on to the cinema – there's a very good film on' – a flight of fancy, but there was bound to be something spectacular on somewhere – 'we've all been hoping to see it, but we're not all off this evening. Rimada was lucky.' She paused for breath, afraid she had overdone it. She had, for he said softly:

'A commendable effort, dear girl, laid on thick with a trowel, just as though you had something to hide. Now what should I do? Go along to the restaurant and join her? The other girls wouldn't mind, would they? Where were they going?' He glanced at his watch, apparently deep in thought. 'If you would tell me which cinema, perhaps that would be better. I could pick her up before the show starts.'

Loveday felt the colour oozing from her cheeks. She managed a, 'Oh, yes, well—' and then came to a full stop, her mind a hideous blank.

'Of course, you and I might dine together instead.' His blue eyes surveyed her keenly. 'After all, I only happened to be passing by, as it were, I intended to do no more than spend an hour or so.'

She accepted with an eagerness which blinded her to the lift of his eyebrows and the muscle twitching at the corner of his mouth. Rimada and Terry almost always went to a small restaurant in Soho, not at all the sort of place the Baron would be likely to patronize. By the time they got back surely Rimada and Terry would be safely in the hospital again. 'That would be very nice,' she told him, a little breathless. 'I – I'll go and change.'

She had already locked up; it only remained for her to accompany him down the stairs and leave him in the consultants' room while she went over to the Home. She flung into her room, almost lightheaded with relief at getting out of such an awkward situation. He had said nothing to make her uneasy as they had gone through the hospital, only talked trivialities; the pattern of a man with an evening to waste.

She chose a dress with care, an amber silk jersey with a ruffled collar and tight sleeves, and fussed a little over her shoes and bag. She looked all right, she decided, peering into the mirror; her hair had gone up nicely and she had on a new eye-shadow which suited her. She caught up her coat and made for the door, reminding herself that the reason that she had taken such pains with her appearance was in order to rivet the Baron's attention upon herself and keep his thoughts from Rimada. There was little truth in this praiseworthy idea, but even though she was half aware of this, she was in no state to dispute it. She ran downstairs, a prey to the fear that Rimada and Terry might have come back early and fallen into the Baron's clutches.

He was walking up and down the hospital forecourt, looking genial. She hurried over to him, unable to prevent herself peering anxiously in all directions as she did so, which meant that she missed his grin of pure delight as he watched her. 'You weren't going out this evening, I hope?' he asked her.

She forced her eyes to look calmly ahead. 'No – oh, no. Have you your car?'

'No, not this time – I flew over.' They had reached the gates and he hailed a taxi. He was a man for whom taxis stopped, probably because he was so very large and moreover had the air of someone who expected them to. She got in and squeezed herself into a corner, and missed again his wicked grin. 'I thought we might try a little place in Soho,' he told her. 'Rimada told me about it; she went there once or twice, I believe.'

She clutched her handbag with hands which would have trembled if she had given them the chance. 'Not Soho,' she managed.

He turned to look at her. 'My dear girl, perhaps you have never been there in the evening? During the day it is a little crowded, I imagine, though some of its smaller streets are delightful. You have not been to the Gay Hussar?'

'No.'

'Then let me be the first to take you there. I feel sure that you will like it – you and Rimada have much in common, I imagine, and she was delighted with it.'

Loveday sighed without knowing it and said nothing; relief had bereft her of words. She was almost sure that Rimada and Terry went to a place called – what was it called? She frowned heavily, trying to re-

73

member, and then when she did, smiled widely: Hostaria Romana, that was the place.

The Gay Hussar was a smallish restaurant. The first person she saw as they entered was Rimada, right at the back, and Terry was with her. She glimpsed their rapt profiles as she followed the head waiter to a table – heaven be thanked – on the other side of the room and well out of their line of vision. With commendable promptitude, she elected to sit so that the Baron would have his broad back towards his cousin – but perhaps he had already seen her? After an age of seconds during which she waited for him to make some remark to that effect, she ventured to look at him. His expression was blandly inquiring, no more than that. He said merely: 'Well, here we are in Soho – I hope you will find that I didn't persuade you to come in vain.'

He hadn't persuaded her at all – just brought her along with him, but she let that pass; no point in annoying him now.

'I'm hungry, I hope you are.' He smiled at her as he spoke with such charm that it brought an answering curve to her pretty mouth. Besides, blessed relief was flooding over her; he hadn't seen Rimada, and if the girl had the sense to stay where she was until they left the restaurant, he never would. Paralysed by the strength of the feelings she had suffered, she came alive once more. 'I'm hungry too,' she told her companion, casting round in her head for a topic of conversation which would keep him interested for the next hour or so.

She talked through the starters, got her second wind

with the smoked duck and was well into her stride with the dessert, a delicate mousse. And under the impression that it would give her courage if anything were to go wrong, she allowed her glass to be filled and re-filled with the excellent hock the Baron had chosen. By the time they had reached the coffee she was feeling gay and slightly pot-valiant. Once or twice she had contrived to peep round her host's massive shoulders, and once she had encountered Rimada's pale, petrified gaze. She had looked away immediately, scared that the Baron might have noticed something, but it seemed that he hadn't, he was signalling the waiter to re-fill their glasses. She took a thankful gulp and felt a fresh wave of courage course through her as she plunged once more into lighthearted chatter, calculated to engage his attention until the end of their meal.

They had finished and she was beginning to worry about leaving before Rimada became too impatient, when he solved the problem for her by remarking gently: 'Much though I am enjoying your – er – unexpectedly gay company, I feel that I should take you back to the Royal City – I expect you have a busy day before you in the morning.'

Loveday was getting out of her chair almost before he had finished speaking and making smartly for the door, hardly pausing to put on the coat held for her. The desire to turn round and look at Rimada was very great; she kept her eyes in front of her however. and thus, for the third time that evening, missed the expression on the Baron's face. Possibly if she had seen it, she might have been forewarned, as it was she climbed into the taxi, and still talking, a little feverishly by now, was conveyed back to the hospital. She would have bidden him good-bye at the entrance, but he got out first, paid off the driver and walked, without being asked, with her across the courtyard to the entrance.

It was very quiet, the only bright lights were coming from the porter's lodge and the Accident Room entrance; the ward lights were out by now, replaced by the soft glow of the night lights. Loveday paused at the door, anxious by now to wish her escort good night. Any moment now Rimada and Terry, thinking themselves safe, might come into the courtyard. But the Baron seemed not to notice her held-out hand, instead he tucked an arm in hers and walked with her through the hospital and across the inner yard until they reached the door of the Nurses' Home.

'Thank you for a very pleasant evening,' she said without wasting time. 'I – I liked Soho after all.'

'You surprise me,' the Baron's voice was horribly silky. 'I had the impression that you were on tenterhooks throughout dinner – indeed, I began to fear that the unusually large quantities of hock which you drank – presumably to help you keep your nerve – would send you under the table. Certainly it sent your tongue rattling in a manner the like of which I haven't heard for many a long year.'

She stared up at his face in the dim light, her blood slowly congealing with fright. At last she managed in a voice which she strove to keep cool and offhand: 'I can't think what you're talking about, Professor de Wolff.

'I don't suppose you can, not after all that hock. I'll refresh your memory for you. you saw my tiresome cousin as soon as we entered the restaurant, did you not? And just because I didn't remark upon her presence, you were little fool enough to suppose that I hadn't seen her. My poor, foolish Miss Pearce, pitting your wits against mine; you'll know better next time.' He laughed, a sound which did nothing to reassure her. 'Now I can say that I enjoyed my evening enormously, watching you toss off glass after glass of wine, and listening to the ceaseless chatter which I suppose you thought would divert my attention from anything else. It was a splendid effort, dear girl, you must be worn out, certainly you will have a shocking headache in the morning.'

He took a step nearer and laid his hands on her shoulders, staring down at her. 'It would be a fitting end to the evening if I were to kiss you.' He thought about it for a long moment. 'But on second thoughts, I don't think I will.'

She felt herself turned smartly and pushed, quite gently, through the door he had opened. As it swung to behind her, she heard his mocking 'Good night, Loveday Pearce,' but she didn't look round. She ran upstairs as hard as she could go, suddenly in tears. It wasn't until she was in bed ten minutes later that she admitted to herself that she wasn't crying over the awful fiasco of an evening, but because the Baron hadn't wanted to kiss her.

She was late for breakfast the next morning, and just as the Baron had so hatefully predicted, she had a headache. When Rimada, late herself, came to sit beside her to drink a hasty cup of tea, she said urgently: 'Rimmy, not now – I've a vile headache.'

Rimada took no notice, but: 'He saw us, didn't he? How could you let him take you to the Gay Hussar? We were there,' she added just as though Loveday didn't know it already.

'Oh, don't be silly,' snapped Loveday, weighed down by headache. 'I had no idea ... you always go to that other place with the funny name. He came to the theatre just as I was going off duty, and wanted to know where you were. So I said you'd gone out – I didn't exactly tell a lie, but I let him think that you'd gone to the flicks with some of the other girls, so he invited me to go out with him instead, and it seemed a good idea because it would keep him occupied and there would be less chance of you meeting.'

Her friend gave her a grateful look, tinged with bewilderment. 'But what did he say?'

Loveday thought. The conversation outside the Nurses' Home was still unpleasantly clear in her head. 'Nothing,' she said at length. 'He just said – when we got back here – that he had seen you, that was all.'

'All?' There was a load of disbelief in Rimada's voice. 'Is he still here?'

'How should I know?' Loveday swallowed her tea and got to her feet. 'And what is more,' she added forcefully, 'I don't care. I must go, Rimmy; there's a colossal list. See you later.' She hurried away, her aching head already full of the morning's problems.

She had no time to worry about the whereabouts of

the Baron after that; she was eating a long-delayed supper at the end of a long, busy day when she saw Rimada again.

'There you are.' said her friend. 'I had my supper hours ago.'

'Naturally,' said Loveday sourly. 'I would have had mine too, only a perf. came in just as we'd finished the list. Sometimes I wonder why I stick it.'

'Well, don't. Get married – like me.' Rimada had recovered her usual aplomb. 'I've been thinking, that pale blue dress would do beautifully to get married in – that gorgeous hat goes very well with it.'

But for once Loveday had very little interest in clothes. 'Did you find out if your guardian had gone?' she wanted to know.

Rimada shrugged. 'I'm sure he has; I telephoned Mama this afternoon and she was expecting him to call this evening – some business he has to attend to for her.' She hesitated. 'Loveday, I told her about Terry.'

Loveday's spoon, loaded with prunes and custard, halted in mid-air.

'Rimmy, you didn't! It's still a week before we go – supposing he gets to hear about it? Your mother . . .'

'She will not tell, wild horses will not drag it from her,' exclaimed Rimada dramatically. 'She will also send more money. There is a good hotel in Funchal, she tells me, it is called Reid's – she wishes us to stay there after we are married.'

Loveday agreed a little absentmindedly. 'You'll need all the money you can get if you're going to stay there for any length of time,' she observed. 'But

Rimmy, why did you have to tell your mother? You promised that you wouldn't until we were on the point of leaving.'

'I know, but then I thought how nice it would be if we had some more money – money is important,' said Rimada simply.

Loveday poured herself a cup of tea. She felt very tired, the illogical thought that it would be nice to pour out her troubles into the Baron's broad shoulder and leave him to sort them out crossed her mind. It was a pity she had promised not to breathe a word to anyone.

She wasn't sure what she expected to happen during those last few days, but nothing did. Even waiting on the docks to go aboard, she found herself glancing round in a stealthy fashion, expecting to see the Baron emerge from the crowds around them. They were on their own, for Terry had decided that it would be better for him to join them on board and not before. Loveday, seeing neither hair nor hide of him, wondered if he had decided not to come at the last moment, and found herself hoping that this might be the case.

It wasn't. He was waiting for them in the ship's foyer, looking handsome and definitely furtive. Loveday, studying his good looks, decided that his chin was too weak, but watching her friend greeting him with extravagant delight, she squashed her doubts; possibly he was exactly the sort of husband Rimada wanted, and who was she to dispute the fact? She wandered away tactfully until she judged they had time enough to talk to each other, and then quietly took charge, for neither of them had given much thought to the actual arrangements once they were on board. Terry she sent to his cabin with the promise that they would meet him in one of the ship's bars in an hour's time, reminding him at the same time that he must visit the Purser's office and secure them a table. Rimada she swept along with her to their own cabin, a comfortable apartment on the sun-deck. Here she calmed her companion's exuberant chatter, obtained a calming tray of tea and set about unpacking. The hour stretched to an hour and a half because Rimada, having changed her dress once, decided to wear something quite different after all, despite Loveday telling her that there was no need for her to change at all that evening. She herself was still wearing the plain pink sheath she had worn under a light coat and beyond redoing her hair and face, had made no great efforts with her appearance; that she had left to Rimada, who was, after all, the heroine of the occasion.

'You look super,' she told her friend as they made their way down to the promenade deck. 'That's a lovely dress.'

Rimada smoothed the skirt of the very pale blue silk poplin she had decided to wear and turned a happy face to her. 'Terry likes me in blue,' she confided happily.

They joined a rather impatient man presently, and had a drink before going in to dinner. The restaurant was vast and lavishly decorated and already almost full. Rather to Loveday's surprise the Chief Steward met them at the door and led them to a table for four in the centre; she must have been mistaken in thinking that Terry had said that the only table he had been able to get had been one at the side of the restaurant, and that for six persons. She wondered who the fourth would be, and hoped there would be no one. The Chief Steward had seated them, and their table steward was already hovering with the menus, when his superior, hurrying as much as his dignity permitted, left them to escort someone else – the Baron, strolling along behind him, making for their table. Rimada had gone the colour of the tablecloth and Terry had sprung to his feet with the air of someone who intended to take cover at once, only there was nowhere for him to go. Loveday eyed Rimada's guardian warily. Had some awful chance brought him here, or had he planned it all? She thought probably the latter. His face gave nothing away – pleased surprise, judging from the gentle smile curving his mouth, but it could have been a smile of satisfaction, too. And there was a far from gentle gleam in his eye. She held her tongue and waited for him to speak.

CHAPTER FIVE

The Baron seated himself with the air of someone who is sure of his welcome, and beamed at them all.

'Now this is a pleasure,' he assured them cordially. 'What an extraordinary coincidence that we should meet like this.' His blue eyes swept the table and rested upon Terry. He extended a great arm, to crush that young man's hand in a grip to make him wince. 'And you? You must be Rimada's future husband. What a splendid opportunity for us to discuss the matter!' He turned a bland face to Loveday, watching him in fascination. 'These young people are so impatient, are they not, Loveday?' His voice held all the qualities of a benevolent uncle.

She was annoyed and amused now as well as deeply apprehensive. The annoyance, for the moment, was uppermost; maybe she was past her first youth, but there was no need for him to include her amongst the middle-aged – and to be told so before an audience. But the audience wasn't listening; it sat in a trance, eyes fixed on the Baron in a kind of fascinated horror.

'I always feel that companions on a holiday of this sort make it so much more enjoyable,' he told the table at large, apparently unaware that he was the only one enjoying himself, and having uttered this palpably false remark, he summoned the steward.

Loveday buried her delightful nose in the menu; she

had been pleasantly hungry, now she had no appetite any more. She stared at the enormous variety of delicious foods she might choose, and would gladly have settled for bread and water. She took so long that the Baron said pleasantly: 'It is difficult to decide, isn't it? Will you let me choose for you?'

She said: 'Thank you, if you would,' and watched him silently while he studied his own menu. He was up to something; he was behaving so out of character that she suspected him of some devious plan. How had he found out that they were aboard the ship in the first place? They had been very careful not to mention its name, nor had they told him the date upon which they were sailing. She had already dismissed the long arm of coincidence as ridiculous. He must have visited Rimada's mother and that silly lady had said something to make him suspicious and he had pounced. She turned her attention to the other two members of the party and found them engrossed in their own menus and quite obviously thinking hard; she hoped their thoughts ran on the same lines as her own and that they would say nothing rash. It was a pity none of them had the faintest idea how much he knew.

But she had no need to worry; the Baron, an urbane and polished man of the world, made no mention of any personal matters; his talk was all of the ship in which they found themselves, the delights of Madeira and Lisbon, both of which places he had already visited. He even complimented Rimada on her appearance, spoiling it rather by adding:

'But you should avoid that wishy-washy blue, my

dear, you're too big a girl to wear it,' and turning to Terry, who had said almost nothing throughout the meal: 'You must agree with me, I feel sure – probably you will be able to persuade her once you are married.' He allowed his eyes to rest upon Loveday. 'Pink,' he mused aloud, 'now pink is such a kind colour.'

She itched to throw a plate at him.

They spent an uneasy evening, sitting in one of the lounges, drinking their after dinner coffee, and because Rimada and Terry seemed incapable of carrying on any sort of a conversation, Loveday found herself sustaining the talk with the Baron, who as the evening advanced became strangely loquacious about his ward's affairs.

'You must make the most of this trip,' he told her kindly.' I hadn't intended telling you just yet, but since your future is settled and you will have Terry to look after you, there is no point in concealing the disagreeable fact that the family fortunes have suffered badly just recently. Investments, I'm afraid.' He entered into a lengthy symposium about stocks and shares, giltedged securities and the like, none of which made sense to his listeners; the only thing which made sense was the fact that Rimada wasn't a rich girl any longer. 'I'm sorry,' he told her in a voice which didn't sound sorry at all.

It was Loveday who had the temerity to ask: 'And you, Professor de Wolff, does this affect you as well?'

His eyes were as guileless as a child's. 'Ah, but I have my profession, have I not? I need never starve.' He gave a cheerful laugh. 'Nor for that matter need

Rimada – there will probably be a small annuity for her, and Terry will be able to support her.'

'But Rimada will need more than that,' thought Loveday worriedly. She had always been used to having exactly what she wanted, when she wanted it, and that wouldn't be possible on Terry's income; he hadn't even got his Fellowship, and somehow she thought he never would. For any other girl, of course, it would be possible – a clear picture of herself, managing very well indeed on the Baron's income, running that large and lovely house on a shoestring with the minimum of help, bringing up a healthy brood of children; entertaining cleverly for him on next to nothing, even making her own clothes – knitting his sweaters, the children's socks, floated before her eyes. She was so engrossed in it that when the Baron spoke to her, he was forced to repeat himself.

'I'm sure you will agree with me, Loveday?'

She looked at him guiltily, imagining in the silliest way that he had been sharing her thoughts. To make up for it, she said in an austere voice: 'I can hardly judge.' She was getting heartily sick of being used as a referee, she would do something about it. 'I'm very tired,' she told him. 'You'll not mind if I go to bed – Rimmy's tired too . . . a long day.'

'And all its attendant worries,' he finished for her in a voice much too smooth for her liking. The men got to their feet, but when Terry made to go as well, the Baron said quickly: 'My dear chap, have another drink, and perhaps we might have that little talk . . .'

Loveday thought that for one moment Rimada was

going to sit down again. She pinched her hard and propelled her down the lounge and along to their cabin and shut the door firmly behind them. 'Don't dare burst into tears, Rimmy,' she urged her friend. 'Let's sit down and think this out. You know, I wouldn't be surprised if Adam doesn't consent to you getting married after all. You see, if you haven't much money left, he'll be glad to get you settled.' She sat down. 'How much does he know?'

'I don't know,' Rimada choked back a sob. 'I don't want to be poor,' she wailed.

'You won't be exactly poor,' Loveday said bracingly. 'Doctors earn enough to live on, you know, and you heard Adam say that there would be an annuity for you – even a few hundred pounds a year will be useful.'

Rimada stamped a foot in its expensive Charles Jourdan shoe. 'I do not wish it to be useful,' she snapped. 'I like to spend money.'

'Well, you'll still be able to do that, but on a smaller scale,' counselled Loveday. 'Look, you've had a shock, Rimmy, but it will be better in the morning when you've slept on it.'

Which turned out to be true enough; Rimada was cheerful after a good night's sleep, she even made one or two plans while they dressed: a small house somewhere in London where they could entertain their friends and from where Terry would go forth each day to some vague position in hospital; not for long, of course, she explained, for he would quickly become a consultant and have his own rooms, and they would be able to move somewhere really fashionable. She chattered on, and Loveday, while deploring her friend's unrealistic approach to life, was too kind-hearted to damp her high spirits. No doubt it would all work out; all the same she would get hold of the Baron and talk to him, it should be easy enough.

It wasn't easy at all; the Baron proved, for a man of such bulk, singularly elusive. Not that he wasn't there; they all met before breakfast and walked round the gently heaving deck, but beyond a pleasant good morning, he showed no desire to seek her company – indeed, he walked off with his cousin, leaving her to talk to Terry, who still looked furtive but for some reason seemed eager to please her. They met again for breakfast, however, after which meal, during which the Baron had displayed the same benevolence as he had done on the previous evening, he excused himself on the grounds of catching up on some reading, only to appear after an hour and whisk Rimada away once more.

It was a big ship. Loveday excused herself in her turn from the now boring Terry, and went looking for the other two, without success. They were in none of the bars or lounges, nor were they in the swimming pools or on the sports deck, she drew a blank in the library too; it was almost lunchtime when she turned a corner of the promenade deck and saw the Baron leaning over the rail, by himself.

'Where's Rimada?' she demanded of him without any polite overtures.

He turned his head to smile at her. 'My dear good

88

girl, you sound like a nursemaid searching for a small child! Rimtsje is with her young man, I imagine.'

'They've hardly seen each other the whole morning,' she began, and then remembered that it was more than an hour since she had left Terry; Rimada might have returned only minutes after she had left him.

'That's right,' encouraged her companion. 'Don't be too hasty, dear girl, second thoughts are often best.'

Loveday refused to be drawn into an argument about thoughts. 'Look,' she uttered quickly before she lost her nerve, 'I've been trying to get you alone all the morning,' and was brought to a halt by his murmured: 'I am indeed flattered, dear girl,' but she decided to ignore this and plunged on: 'Even if Rimmy hasn't any money, you will give her a decent wedding, won't you, and let her stay at Reid's. All her plans – it would break her heart. You wouldn't understand, of course, men don't, but the hardest part for her was making up her mind to a quiet wed . . .' She stopped, aware all at once of what she was saying. Rimada might have told him everything, but then again she might not, and what made it worse was that it was impossible to tell what he knew from his reply.

'Oh, I'm not a pauper, you know. She may have any kind of a wedding she wants within reason.' He stared down at her, his mouth lifting a little at the corners. 'And what sort of wedding would you like, Loveday?'

'Me?' She was still recovering; at least he hadn't seemed to notice anything unusual; Rimada might have told him after all that she and Terry were planning to get married when they got to Madeira; it was terrible not knowing. 'I don't know,' she said carefully. 'I don't think I'd mind if it were quiet, I'd feel more married then.' She remembered something then and added with a decided sparkle in her brown eyes: 'Besides, I'm a bit long in the tooth to wear white satin and orange blossom.'

His laughter was unexpected and annoyed her. 'Even when you grind your teeth at me you're beautiful,' he told her. 'One day you'll make a lovely bride.'

'We're talking about Rimada,' she reminded him, and leaned over the rail to watch the blue waters of the Bay of Biscay. She felt his arm across her shoulders with a thrill of pleasure. His shoulder was firm behind hers; it was strange, she mused silently, how one felt safe with some people – more than safe. She made to move a little away, but his arm tightened so that she found it impossible. 'A pity no one tells me anything,' he said softly.

'But someone has – they must have done, otherwise how . . . Rimada's mother, she told you!'

'Discerning girl. Only by accident, you know. My aunt is charming, she is also a little foolish. That didn't matter while my uncle was alive, because he loved her very dearly and she did exactly as he told her. Rimada is very like her mother.' He sighed. 'It is a pity that she would not tell me the whole tale – I was forced to put two and two together and make five.' His voice took on a silky note and she, afraid that he was about to make good his ignorance at her expense, exclaimed hastily and with no truth whatever: 'Oh, look – porpoises!'

The rest of the day was pleasant enough, it surprised her how quickly her fears became lulled by the charm of the Baron's manner; no mention was made of weddings, futures or loss of fortunes, they spent the day taking part in the various activities laid on for the passengers' entertainment, lunched gaily and dined still more gaily, and afterwards they danced in the vast ballroom. Only Loveday found that for most of the time she had Terry for a partner. Getting ready for bed later that night, she mentioned this a little diffidently to Rimada and was surprised to find that she didn't mind at all. 'Adam has a lot to discuss with me,' she explained. 'He has promised me a lovely wedding.'

'Rimmy, does he know? I mean about you and Terry getting married in Madeira?'

'Yes, I told him.'

Loveday sat down on her bed and began to brush her hair. 'And Terry?'

Rimada looked faintly worried. 'He says that it is impossible to make plans until we arrive there.' She was sitting before the looking glass trying her hair out in a new style. 'You like this?' she wanted to know.

The next two days were much as the first, only it was warmer now. The girls wore cotton dresses and joined the men in the swimming pool each morning. It was a delightful life, a little lazy perhaps, but a pleasant change from the hurry and ordered bustle of hospital life, but its perfection was marred for Loveday at least by the uncertainty of the future. She found to her annoyance that she had far too much of Terry's company

– indeed, he was showing signs of a friendliness which she didn't much care for, something she was unable to say of the Baron, who treated her with the cool courtesy of a good host determined to be civil at all costs. She found this attitude hard to put up with, but not as hard as the air of benevolence which he extended to all three of them. But Rimada seemed content enough, although she had once or twice voiced vague doubts about being a poor man's wife, but as she never listened to Loveday's comments on this, Loveday was forced to the conclusion that the doubts weren't very strong. She had the unhappy feeling that they were suspended in a vacuum waiting for someone to tell them what to do next, the someone being the Baron.

She wakened early on the fourth morning to find that they were steaming slowly into the harbour at Funchal. It was going to be a glorious day; the pale sky, still clouded at its corners by the last of the night; the white-walled, red-roofed houses of the town taking on the colour of the sun's rays creeping over the horizon – it was quite beautiful, but she couldn't see enough from their cabin. She pulled on her dressing gown, stuck her feet into her slippers and, after a vain effort to waken Rimada, went on deck; she hadn't come thousands of miles to miss anything as magnificent as this.

The town spread itself before her, its narrow waterfront stretching along the coast, while the houses and churches of the town behind it climbed higher and higher into the great grey mountains behind. How did one reach the top, she wondered, and once there, how did one get down again? The town petered away on either side, in one direction to grey rocks which in turn had, in some bygone age, cascaded into the sea and formed rocky islands, a little grim even in the lovely light. But on the other side the houses, although fewer, were larger, and spaced out along the cliffs and into the mountains. Hotels, she guessed; it would be nice to stay in one of them. She turned to watch the sun and found that the Baron had come silently to stand beside her. He was in slacks and an open-necked shirt; moreover, he was freshly shaved; his impeccable appearance reminded her that her hair was hanging down her back in an early morning tangle and her face hadn't been washed. Her, 'Good morning; Professor de Wolff,' was in consequence a little stiff with shyness. He appeared to have no eyes for her; his own greeting was brief and casual as he studied the scene before them.

'This is worth coming to see, isn't it?' he wanted to know, and leaned over the rail with the air of a man who had come to stay.

'It's quite beautiful,' she agreed, suddenly wholly at ease. 'I've been wondering how people could live right up those mountains – there's surely no way of getting a car up there?'

'A number of the streets from the town run back into the mountains, though you can't see them easily from here, but on the island itself there are very few roads; one right round the coast, and another two running south to north through the mountain passes. They're quite good as long as you don't do more than fifteen miles an hour and don't mind hairpin bends.'

'You've been on them?'

'Oh, yes.' She waited for him to say more, but he wasn't a man to talk about himself.

'It's volcanic, isn't it?' she hazarded.

'Yes. By the way, I've hired a car for the day, you will be able to see something of the island later on.' He looked about him. 'I should think that we might go ashore about eight o'clock. Perhaps you could get Rimada to wake up – she takes so long to dress – tell her to put on something pretty.'

He turned away, leaving her standing surprised. Why on earth should he bother with what Rimada wore? He said over his shoulder, 'You had better do the same, although you look very nice like that.'

He had disappeared before she could frame an answer.

Rimada, once wakened and warned of the day's programme, dressed with commendable speed. It was as they hurried down to breakfast that Loveday asked: 'Rimmy, what happens now? We're here, in Madeira – you were going to get married.'

But all she got for an answer was, 'Terry must think of something.' The Dutch girl looked at her thoughtfully. 'Adam isn't cross any more, you know.'

It was on the tip of Loveday's tongue to say that of course he wasn't; he had had his own way, hadn't he? He had driven a wedge, almost not to be noticed, between the happy pair, and furthermore, neither of them seemed to mind. She was still puzzling about this when they got to the breakfast table.

It was still very early and the Baron had been right;

94

by eight o'clock those who wished might go ashore, Rimada disappeared to fetch a straw hat, and Loveday, who hadn't brought one with her, was left on deck with the two men. She was barely out of sight when the Baron, telling Terry to wait for Rimada, took Loveday by the arm and walked her off the ship.

There were several people standing about, looking at the merchandise arranged on the dockside; basket work, embroidery, straw hats, tablecloths, bedspreads – a colourful collection of hand work to tempt the tourist. Loveday was on the point of telling her companion that she would like a closer look when he came to a halt. There was a man coming towards them, as tall as the Baron but of much slimmer build. He had a craggy face with blunt features which broke into a smile as he saw them.

'Adam!' he exclaimed. '*Dag, jongen*, it's good to see you – here I am as you suggested, though it was difficult enough.' He gave Adam an enquiring look as he spoke.

'She's coming,' said the Baron quietly. 'This is Guake ten Kate, Loveday – a friend of mine, and of Rimada.'

Loveday shook hands. So this was the future; she thought she saw it all now; a pity there was no time to ask questions, but the other two had joined them and Rimada had flung herself at Guake with the happy familiarity of an old friend. The Baron watched them, looking smug, as well he might, thought Loveday savagely. He had arranged everything very nicely; if Guake wasn't a devoted admirer of Rimada, guaranteed to get her away from Terry, she herself was a blind fool. She began a conversation with Terry, although she didn't want to, but he looked neglected and decidedly sullen, but the Baron broke up Rimada's happy chatter with a cheerful: 'Well, come on, everyone – the car's over here.'

He swept everyone along with no effort at all. Loveday found herself in the back seat with Terry between her and Rimada, while Guake got in beside the Baron. It wasn't long before she was envying them; Rimada for some reason was not only excited, she was sulky too, a combination of feelings which made rational conversation impossible. Moreover, Terry had tried to hold her hand – she pushed it away impatiently and looking up saw the Baron watching them in the driving mirror, a circumstance which caused her to embark on several remarks about the scenery in an unnaturally high voice.

'Delightful,' declared her host. 'Bananas, as you can see, grapes too. If you look to the left you will see Reid's Hotel and the sea beyond. We're going back there later on.'

They were climbing steadily, following the road running parallel to the sea, passing through small villages whose tiny houses and bigger villas looked very picturesque. Loveday, a practical girl, while acknowledging their charm, wondered about indoor sanitation and the water supply, but was soon diverted by the sight of the flowers, growing vividly over every wall; bright blue convolvulus, red and yellow hibiscus and red bougainvillea.

'Camara de Lobos,' explained the Baron as they swept into a village. 'Rather nice, don't you think? Look at the fishing boats below.' And a few minutes later: 'Isn't it remarkable how they can cultivate such steep ground, right to the edge – they must like heights.'

He turned to speak to Guake in their own language and Loveday endeavoured to engage her companions in conversation, without much success. She had never known Rimada so thoughtful, and as for Terry, when she caught his eye he smiled at her with such warmth that she was filled with uneasiness. She looked out of the window again; they were still climbing, with the mountains towering on one side and the sea on the other, far below. They must be very high by now. She said so to no one in particular and Guake said over one shoulder: 'Wait just a few minutes more, then there is really something to see.'

The road wound up and up and suddenly turned and ran straight for the sea, to end in a dirt track which spilled itself on to an enormous balcony.

'Everyone out!' cried the Baron cheerfully. Just as though he had a merry, friendly party aboard, thought Loveday, ignoring his hand as he opened the door, and walking with the others to the stone balustrade ahead of them.

Too late she realized that they were about to look down from a great height on to the rocky coast and the sea, almost two thousand feet below. With a mouth gone dry, she edged away, turned round, walking carefully rather as though she were balancing something on her head, her eyes fixed on a remote, safe spot in the mountains, and began to move away from the terrifying edge. She had taken perhaps a dozen trembling steps when the Baron's hand jerked her to a halt. 'My dear girl,' he began, 'you're missing the best.'

'I do not like heights,' said Loveday coldly, her voice shaking ever so slightly, her eyes still fixed on the mountains, aware that by now she was probably a nasty green colour.

The hand became all at once protective and gentle. 'Loveday – I didn't know, you must forgive me. Rimada adores this sort of thing, I never guessed that you wouldn't . . . she's hanging over the cliff now with Guake holding her safe.'

Loveday suppressed a strong shudder. She knew that he was looking at her and with a great effort withdrew her eyes from the heights beyond and looked at him instead. His face was full of concern; sometimes she had been out with people who had laughed at her terror of heights, but he wasn't laughing; he understood. She relaxed a little and he said at once: 'That's better. Don't look anywhere but in front of you – there's a dirt track on the left, between the trees. I'll walk on the outside so that you can look around you, you won't see anything there, it's completely screened.'

He was walking her along without haste, talking of nothing much, and presently she had her nerve back again and was able to say: 'I'm sorry, I do despise myself for being such a coward.'

'There's nothing cowardly about it; acrophobia is a

condition of which you need not be ashamed.' He smiled down at her, her arm tucked firmly into his.

'Look round you now, there are only trees.'

His voice was kind; it was strange, thought Loveday, how it affected her; she would have liked to have told him her doubts about Rimada and Terry. Upon reflection, she would have liked to have told him a great many things – silly little things, which he would probably laugh at – no, he would never laugh, she was sure of that. She pulled her thoughts up sharply. This would never do; she was beginning to think too much about him. There would be more sense in asking a few questions.

'You arranged for Mr. ten Kate to be here?' she asked. 'You knew all about Rimmy and Terry, didn't you? How did you manage to cool them off?'

'You're observant. Yes, I got Guake to get here before us. He has loved Rimada for a very long time, ever since she had plaits, and for that reason she had always accepted him as someone very safe and certain, always there, but never really seeing him. She is a silly girl but a nice one, she will make him a very good wife.'

'Aren't you going a little fast?'

'No, I merely look ahead. I must admit that it took me a little time and a good deal of trouble to get to the bottom of this muddle, and you hardly helped.'

She let this pass. 'And Terry? I'm tired of Terry,' she stated, suddenly waspish, her fears all gone by now. 'He haunts me. I don't even like him, and anyway, he's in love with Rimada.'

'You mistake, dear girl,' his voice was suave. 'He's in love with her money – indeed, he is able to fix his affections upon any girl with money.' Something in his voice made her glance at him; he was regarding her with a quizzical lift of the eyebrows and his eyes were alight with laughter.

She stared back, her eyes enormous in a still green-white face. 'That wasn't true about Rimmy losing her money, was it? I might have guessed. You said that to put him off – to test him . . .'

He was smiling gently. 'Go on, dear girl,' he begged her.

Her mouth dropped open with sudden shock. 'You – you . . .' she began. 'Why, that's why he's been so repulsively friendly, he thought – what did you tell him?'

'Only that you were an heiress. A distant uncle, you know.'

She stamped her foot in its pretty sandal. 'You're abominable! I've never heard anything like it, you've just done exactly what you wanted to do – riding roughshod . . .' Laughter bubbled up inside her, although she wanted to cry at the same time. The laughter won and he said quietly:

'I hoped you would do that. I knew I could count on your sense of humour.'

'Well, don't,' she told him furiously, the laughter gone, leaving an unpleasant feeling behind it; he had made use of her, just as she had no doubt that he would make use of anyone if he wished to do so.

'I laughed about it,' she told him, 'but even though it

was funny, I – I don't like you for doing it. You had no right . . .' She swallowed back a hard ball of tears in an angry way, keeping her eyes wide and determinedly dry.

They were standing in the middle of the dirt track; the sun, very warm now, filtered by the trees arched over them. The Baron sounded humble. 'No, I had no right, you will have to forgive me for that; there was no time to do anything else.'

She answered reluctantly, 'No, I suppose there wasn't. Is Rimada going to stay here?'

He took her hands in his in an absent-minded fashion. 'I think that we shall all stay here. Guake has got rooms for us at Reid's. I arranged for your steward-ess to pack your things, and they will be at the hotel by the time we arrive.'

Loveday tugged at her hands to get them free, but he held them fast.

'How dare you? It just so happens that I want to finish the cruise, that's what we had planned. It's – it's . . .' She stopped, at a loss for words.

'Listen, Loveday. Rimada will go back to Holland with me – I have booked a flight for a couple of days' time, and Guake will naturally stay with us and return on the same flight. I don't know about the unfortunate Terry – I very much doubt if he spent his own money on this trip.' He saw the look on Loveday's face. 'I thought not. You must stay too, for Rimada's sake – besides, I want her to be with Guake as much as pos-sible, that will be easier if there are four of us.' He grinned down at her. 'Do you not say, "Two is company, three is none?" You must agree with me that he will make her a very good husband, anyone can see that at a glance.'

'But my holiday . . .'

'Of course, if you wish, you could continue your cruise, I'm sure Terry will be delighted – think of the opportunities he will have.'

She threw him a look of dislike. 'How horrid you are! I'll stay, but there is one thing, you'll have to pay my hotel bill because I believe it's a most expensive place and I haven't a great deal of money with me, but I shall be obliged if you will send me the amount I owe you when I get back to London.'

'Anything you say, dear girl.' His voice was so meek that she cast him a look of suspicion.

'And I wanted to see Lisbon,' she remembered.

'That will be easy – we fly to Lisbon and spend a night there before going on to Holland. I give you my word that you shall crowd as much sightseeing as can be managed into our stay there.' He pulled her to him and kissed her cheek gently. 'You are a kind girl, and after all, it is for Rimada's happiness.' He tucked her hand into his. 'Now we will return to the car and this time you shall sit between Guake and Rimada and then you will feel safe. I will have Terry with me.' They began to walk slowly back the way they had come.

'What will you tell him?' she wanted to know, 'and when?'

He only answered part of her question. 'We'll stop for coffee, you three can go for a stroll, or he and I will take a walk – don't worry about it.'

'You won't be nasty?'

'Nasty?' He had stopped to stare at her. 'Nasty? Certainly not; he has his pride of sorts, presumably; I won't puncture it. I thought you didn't like him?'

'I don't, but he's got nothing, has he? I mean, Rimada and her money and a future.'

'He never had them – and he's having a delightful holiday at no cost to himself.' He sounded contemptuous.

They were almost at the car. 'And Rimada, does she know that her fortune is safe?'

'Not yet. And if you tell her, Loveday, you will regret it; I will see that you do. Being without money may help her to see Guake in a new light; it may humble her a little, too.'

'You're a hard man,' observed Loveday.

'Perhaps I am, but not always and not with everyone. I could never be hard towards you; you're too good an opponent.'

His words struck a chill into her bones; she had forgotten that they had been on opposite sides, and apparently they still were. She got into the car telling herself that she had only herself to thank for it.

ing the villa. She even almost convinced herself that it was the wrong reason and hastily shook her head, half smiling. 'You'll need some help to cope with Jason

CHAPTER SIX

WHATEVER the Baron had said to Terry, it couldn't have worried him over-much, for he came back to sit with the rest of them; joining in their conversation while they had their cool drinks, with no sign of discomfort. Only when he had finished did he ask Rimada to stroll down to the harbour with him, leaving the other three to make desultory conversation. It was warm now – too warm for Loveday, the Baron pronounced firmly, and leaving Guake placidly smoking his pipe, he took her across the village square to a row of small shops in its narrow main street.

'You need one of these,' he told her, pausing outside one of the shops where there was a pile of wide-brimmed hats on the pavement, and she obediently picked one up and since it fitted her head, left it on.

'Very pretty,' decided her companion as he pulled out a handful of notes. 'You're the first woman for whom I've bought a hat who didn't spend hours preening in front of a glass.'

The idea of him buying hats for other women was so unusual that Loveday, who had spied a mirror and had been about to study her reflection in it, refrained, while her nicely arched brows drew together in a frown. So he bought hats for his girl-friends, did he? All part and parcel of his being a gay bachelor, just as Rimada had described him. She said coldly: 'Indeed?' and unable to think of anything more telling than this, began to examine some handkerchiefs an old woman was offering her. She was on the point of inquiring how much they were when the Baron asked: 'You find them pretty?' and when she told him yes, handed the old lady some notes and gave her a dozen of the dainty things. 'And before you tell me that you intended to buy them for yourself, may I beg you to accept a trifling souvenir of Madeira, and if that sticks in your throat, then I'll add them to the hotel bill.'

He sounded amused and faintly mocking; there was nothing to do but to thank him nicely, admire the fine embroidery, and stroll on down the street to a shop where she could buy cards to send home. He paid for those too, smiling in a way to cause her to hold her tongue, and then walked on with her while she made suitable remarks about the little town, its shops and the scenery, to be cut short finally by his abrupt:

'We've given them time enough, we'll go back now.'

She could think of nothing sufficiently cutting to say on the spur of the moment in reply to this remark; she had actually believed that he was enjoying her company, instead of which he had been filling in time while Rimada and Terry had the little talk he had so neatly contrived for them. She remained silent until they reached the café again where she seated herself beside the patient Guake and pointedly ignoring the Baron, engaged him in bright chatter, an action which unfortunately was partly wasted, because after only a couple of minutes, he had turned and walked away without a word.

He was back again within five minutes, accompanied by Rimada, looking bewildered and somehow relieved, and Terry, who looked sullen. They all went back to the car, and Terry, contriving to get close to Loveday as they crossed the square, astonished her by saying in a low voice:

'You could have told me that you're to be married soon.'

Before she could deny this remarkable statement, the Baron was between them, telling them with a wealth of unnecessary detail where they were going next. 'And then the hotel, I think,' he boomed genially, 'and luncheon before we take Terry back to the ship.' He took care too, that no one should have a chance for a tête-à-tête, for when Loveday suggested that she and Rimada should go to their rooms to tidy themselves before the meal, he pointed out, still affable, that they need go no further than the cloakroom close to the hotel restaurant; after lunch was time enough for them to inspect their rooms. So Loveday, balked of her chance to sound Rimada out on the morning's happenings, repaired to the powder room which she found so full of other women that the chance to say even a word was hopeless from the start, and when they returned and the Baron inquired politely if they had found everything to their satisfaction she told him with some asperity that it had been crowded and watched the little satisfied smile on his face with helpless rage.

Lunch, surprisingly enough, turned out to be a very pleasant meal. The Baron bridged the awkward pauses and maintained a flow of small talk with the consummate ease of someone who knew that he had the situation well in hand, and when Terry wished them good-bye with small sign of any regret at the end of their lunch, she was disconcerted with his manner towards Rimada – almost businesslike, she considered, certainly brisk; no one seeing them would have known that only a short time ago the two of them had intended to get married. As for herself, she was treated to another reproachful look and a murmured: 'If you should change you mind, Loveday, you have only to let me know – I shall be waiting.'

He pressed her hand as he spoke and walked away, his head slightly bowed, leaving her staring after him in bewilderment. Anyone would think that it was she and not Rimada who was the object of his disappointed love. Rimada and Guake had already wandered away towards the hotel terrace – surely Rimada might have waited until Terry had gone ... She caught the Baron's eye and found him smiling; the look on his face was that of someone with a job well done. She was still frowning at him when he suggested: 'Why not come with us, Loveday?' and before she could find an excuse, he had opened the door of the car and scooped her neatly into the back seat. Beside Terry.

It was the Baron who chatted pleasantly about this and that as he took them down to the docks. It was the Baron who ushered Terry out of the car, barely giving him time to say good-bye once more. She watched while he went up the gangplank, with the Dutchman blocking its end with his large person, for all the world as though he anticipated that the younger man would turn round and come back again. But he didn't, he waved from the open door of the main deck, and disappeared.

'Did he want to go?' asked Loveday the moment her companion had settled himself beside her after inviting her to come and sit in front.

'What had he to stay for?' demanded the Baron. 'Rimada with no money, and you, an heiress, on the point of marrying – he had the sense to cut his losses.'

She turned a shocked face to his. 'Is that what you told him? That I was going to get married? But I'm not – I have no intention . . .' She drew a deep indignant breath. 'So that's why he told me that if I changed my mind . . .' She let the breath out in what sounded like a snort. 'I never heard anything like it – the nerve . . .'

'Ah, but I'm a surgeon, we need nerve, you know,' he sounded quite undisturbed by her temper. 'Why, I remember once – in Utrecht, or was it Leiden? there was a case . . .'

'I am not in the least bit interested in your cases,' she told him crossly. 'You've behaved abominably!'

He nodded in agreement as he slid the car between the piles of merchandise, the people, and the vehicles which crowded the docks.

'Oh, indeed I have. But in a year – two years, it won't matter a little bit. What will matter is that Rimada and Guake will be happily married, just as they are meant to be.' He glanced at her. 'And you will be married, Loveday, and so, I fancy, shall I.'

Her impulse, at once discouraged, was to ask him

who to. Perhaps he was already engaged. She looked idly around her as they sped along the road towards the hotel. Now if he had been engaged to her, she would never have allowed him to traipse thousands of miles; she would have dissuaded him from going, or better still, gone with him. She remembered that she was still vexed with him and asked. 'And Rimada? Didn't she mind at all – I had no chance to talk to her.' She shot him a baleful look and saw the corner of his mouth twitch in amusement.

They were climbing the hill away from the centre of the town now.

'No, I didn't intend you to; you might have had some well-meaning scheme up your sleeve which would have spoilt everything. Leave her to Guake.' He swung the car through the hotel gates. 'Here we are.'

As he held the door open for her to get out Loveday said tartly: 'I really can't think why I said I'd stay, for you are so rude – I can see that I'm not going to enjoy my holiday in the least.'

He took her arm and walked her round to the terrace overlooking the sea. 'Oh, yes, you are,' he assured her, smiling. 'Sit down, and we'll have a long, cold drink, unless you would prefer tea?' and when they had settled themselves. 'The other two should be along presently, you and Rimtsje can go and unpack what you need for a couple of days.'

She remembered his plans then. 'Yes, but when we get to Lisbon, are we flying on to London, Rimmy and I? We're due to start work . . .'

The drinks came and he handed her something

pleasantly iced in a tall glass. 'You will both be coming back to Holland, to Rimada's home – her mother will be delighted to see you for a few days.' He shot her an amused glance. 'You don't need to worry, unless you wish to, you don't have to see me again once we get to Holland.' His voice was blandly reassuring, which should have pleased her and didn't.

Rimada joined them presently, and Guake with her. She didn't look in the least like a girl who had just parted from a man she had had every intention of marrying, but chattered away until they went upstairs to their rooms; two delightful apartments overlooking the sea, sharing a balcony and a bathroom between them. Loveday, looking around her at the luxury of her surroundings, wondered what it would all cost. How like the Baron, she thought grumpily; just because he had no money problems he would naturally want the best of everything without giving a thought to her own purse – she would be broke for months. Still, as she was here she might as well make the best of things; she unpacked what she considered she might need for the next two days and wandered out on to the balcony and into Rimada's room.

Her friend was sitting at her dressing table, trying out a collection of lipsticks. She gave Loveday a slightly shamefaced look and asked:

'Do you think that I am awful – heartless and selfish?'

Loveday sat down on the bed. 'No. In fact I think it's a good thing that your guardian interfered; you can see now that it wouldn't have worked out. I think,' she went on carefully, 'that one can imagine oneself in love and really believe that it's the real thing, and then one discovers it isn't, and I daresay a great many people don't know how to get out of it and so they get married and are unhappy for ever after.'

'Terry wanted my money.' Rimada was still surprised about this. 'He was glad not to have to marry me when Adam told him that I no longer had any.' She leaned forward to get a better view of her mouth. 'Guake doesn't mind if I am penniless. I have known him all my life, but today it is as if I have seen him for the first time.'

Loveday got up and went to look at the view from the open door. The sun was still delightfully warm, its late afternoon gold made her look prettier than ever. 'Guake's nice,' she said. 'Did he find it awkward coming here without much warning – I mean, he hadn't planned a holiday, had he?'

Rimada, happy about the lipstick at last, joined her on the balcony.

'He came because Adam told him that I would be here.' She went pink. 'He has a regard for me.'

'Well, yes – I thought perhaps he had.' Loveday smiled at her. 'Look, Rimmy, don't think about getting married for a little while, give yourself a chance to get to know Guake properly – oh, I know you've known him for ages, but I wonder how well? And let him get to know you – the part of you who likes babies and stray dogs and lends money to people and never asks for it back and buys flowers for lonely patients – oh, don't look like that, I know all that; he doesn't, but give him the chance to find out. And he will, you'll see.'

'Then you are not annoyed that we stay here instead of staying on the ship? I think that we shall have a good time, and Adam says that he will take us out in Lisbon and Mama will be so glad to have us home for the rest of our holiday.'

'I'm not annoyed,' said Loveday, and was surprised to find that she meant what she was saying, only upon reflection she wasn't sure if she liked the way Adam had arranged the rest of her holiday for her. She debated as to whether she should return to her home instead of going to Rimada's, and rather thought that she would, although she didn't allow this decision to spoil the evening. She put on a long dress of cream and pink chiffon, which, while not in the same class as Rimada's green organza model, certainly enhanced her dark good looks, and accompanied her friend downstairs to the bar where the two men, very sleek and elegant, waited for them.

The evening began delightfully; they dined gaily, a delicious meal which Loveday ate without knowing what it was, aware only that she was enjoying it. And afterwards they danced, and although she started off with Guake as a partner, she very soon found herself with Adam, watching the other two disappear into the hotel grounds.

'Highly satisfactory,' murmured her companion into her ear, 'though I don't suppose that you would agree with me.'

Loveday was an honest girl. 'But I do,' she told him, 'although I don't think you ... that is, you have been very ruthless . . .'

They were idling round the dance floor, and instead of answering her he made some trifling remark about the band which she was forced to answer in kind, much though she wished to remind him once again that his interference had spoilt her holiday. Even as she thought this, she found herself admitting that it wasn't true – her holiday wasn't being spoilt at all. The hotel was perfection itself, she found Madeira enchanting – just as long as she kept away from its appalling clifftops, and as for her companions, was not Rimada her best friend, and was not Guake a perfect dear; the kind of man anyone would get on with from the moment one met him? and as for the Baron –

She experienced a peculiar sensation as she thought about him; her feelings were rapidly undergoing a change towards him. He was infuriating and he liked his own way and he could be nasty when he had a mind to be, but he could also be kind. She looked up into his face at that moment and discovered a look upon it which wasn't in the least kind, only extremely thoughtful, as though he could read her thoughts and was trying to decide what to do about them. She found herself unable to look away, and when he stopped dancing she went on looking at him, standing quiet within his arms while other couples revolved around them. She felt excited, as though something wonderful was about to happen, the excitement suddenly crystallized into a knowledge which rounded her magnificent eyes and caused her pretty mouth to gape slightly. She was in love with this man; it hit her like a sharp blow so that she drew a long breath, searching the blue eyes looking so intently into hers as though she expected a response. But his eyes held nothing but faint amusement.

'You look as though you had forgotten the key to the front door,' he told her lightly. 'Come outside and get sentimental under the moon.'

It couldn't have been worse; Loveday flinched as though she had received a physical hurt, while at the same time she told herself that in the circumstances it was the kind of remark she might have expected – and deserved. After all, she had done everything she could to help Rimada against him, hadn't she? and he had called her an interfering busybody; it was amazing how that rankled still. She said, her voice as light as his: 'By all means, but I'm past the age of getting sentimental, you know, but I daresay the moon will be worth looking at.'

They were on the terrace, watching the moonlit water below before he answered her. 'I deserved that.' He leaned on the balustrade beside her. 'Do you dislike me very much, Loveday?'

And there's a facer, she thought desperately, and wondered what he would say if she were to tell him that she had discovered, only a few moments ago, that she loved him. 'I don't dislike you at all, though I can't think why not; you have annoyed me enough.'

He laughed ruefully. 'Indeed I must have done, but you see I was surprised . . .'

She peered at his face through the deep blue of the late evening. 'Surprised? Why?'

'Never mind. Doesn't Funchal look delightful with all its lights? A charming town, I think – the only large one on the island, though I expect you already know that.'

If he felt like giving her a geography lesson, she hadn't much choice but to listen; presumably it was the alternative to getting sentimental in the moonlight. She had asked for it, she supposed, and asked, quite meekly, if he would tell her something of the island.

She didn't hear a word he said, of course; she was listening to his voice and when there was an opportunity, studying his face, bone white and black-shadowed in the moonlight. He could go on for ever, as far as she was concerned; just being there beside him was enough – for the moment at any rate.

'And now, having talked myself hoarse upon a subject which the pair of us have found exceedingly dull, may I ask what you have been thinking? for you certainly weren't listening.'

'How do you know that?'

He chuckled. 'Because once or twice I spoke Dutch, and you being you, Loveday, wouldn't be likely to let that pass, not if you were paying attention. No, you were deep in thought – not, I hope, more plots against me?'

'No, oh, no.' She was breathless and suddenly quite reckless. 'I think that perhaps the moonlight has made me feel much younger and – and sentimental.'

He turned to look at her. 'An invitation, Miss Pearce?'

The recklessness was still there; she was going to

regret it later on. Now she said steadily: 'Yes.' She had intended to say more, but he had caught her close and was kissing her. There was fierce mockery in the kiss, the mockery was in his voice too. 'There is something rather absurd, dear girl, is there not, in two — er — mature people such as we are allowing ourselves to be carried away by a touch of moonlight and a little too much wine with our dinner.'

She had no idea what to say, she had drawn away from him and perhaps she would have turned and run if Rimada and Guake hadn't joined them at that moment, making it necessary to join in the lighthearted talk for some minutes before they all went back into the hotel. Loveday, longing to be somewhere quiet where she could have a good cry, decided against pleading a headache; it would give the Baron a chance to make one of his nasty remarks. Instead she caught the eye of a fellow guest and smiled at him. She could smile very invitingly when she chose; it helped a little to see the Baron's face as she and the gentleman joined the gay throng on the dance floor. She remained there for some time, getting, if truth must be told, a little tired, and even when she at last made her excuses, she allowed herself to be led to the bar, where she remained for a further ten minutes or so, drinking the vermouth she had been offered and which she loathed, and chattering brightly. She wished her acquaintance goodnight finally, with a half promise to meet him at the swimming pool in the morning, and returned to her own party.

Guake spoke first. 'Nice to see you enjoying yourself,

Loveday,' he observed, and she could see that he actually meant it, but Rimada said in a surprised voice: 'Why, Loveday, I didn't know you were like that.'

'Like what?' The vermouth was going to her head.

'Well, so very . . . your manner was quite . . .'

'Come-hitherish,' supplied the Baron in a voice which had a nasty edge to it. He looked at Loveday and smiled coldly. 'A pattern for me to follow, dear girl?'

The vermouth spoke. 'Not you, Professor de Wolff, perhaps I didn't make that quite clear out on the terrace just now.' She put her elegant head on one side and smiled sweetly at him, longing to burst into tears. 'I wanted to see what you would do – and you did.'

She had a brief glimpse of his blue eyes, blazing down at her. He was very angry; probably girls didn't speak to him like that, and if they did, it would only be the once; they wouldn't get a second chance. She swallowed and asked a shade too brightly: 'Are there any plans for tomorrow?'

It was he who answered her. 'None of importance, so don't let us interfere with any of your own.' His glance flickered towards her erstwhile dancing partner, sitting at the bar. 'You have a date, perhaps?' His voice was casual now, almost friendly; she must have imagined the anger. She made haste to deny any plans of her own and entered enthusiastically into several ideas for the following morning. There was a village up in the hills which really should be visited, she was told. They could drive up there and the two girls if they fancied the idea, could return downhill on a sort of sleigh, very popular with tourists. And after lunch, perhaps a stroll round Funchal. It sounded pleasant and not too arduous, they parted for the night on the friendliest of terms.

Loveday was sitting up in bed brushing out her hair when Rimada came round the balcony to sit on the end of the bed. She began in a satisfied voice: 'I have had a very pleasant day,' and sounded so smug about it that Loveday said rather sharply: 'You might have been married by now.'

Rimada looked conscience-stricken, but only for a moment. 'It would have been a disaster,' she pronounced. 'Adam was right, I see that now. I am definitely not the right wife for a poor man. He considers it noble and unselfish of me to give Terry up without a fuss.'

Loveday choked. 'He said that?' She wondered what he had told Terry; something equally comforting, no doubt. 'You're quite happy to go back to Holland, then, Rimmy?'

The Dutch girl looked surprised. 'But what else should I do? Besides, there is Guake.'

'So there is,' said Loveday dryly. 'Isn't it going to be a little awkward when you get back to the Royal City – with Terry?'

'But I do not go back – Adam will arrange it, he says that it will not do at all. I shall stay at home with Mama.'

'Won't you find that a little dull?'

Rimada had strolled over to the looking glass and

was examining her face carefully. 'Dull? How can that be? And there will be Guake.'

Loveday swallowed a number of things she would have liked to have said and remarked instead: 'Rimmy, you weren't really in love with Terry, were you, only infatuated.'

'You are right – it was romantic, but not very real now that Guake has explained to me what married love should be.' She spoke seriously and then turned back to the glass again. 'I have a spot, does it show very much?'

'You look very pretty,' said Loveday, 'and I can't see any spot.' She couldn't help adding: 'I wonder what Terry's doing now?'

'Finding himself an heiress,' stated Rimada, and there was no regret in her voice at all. Loveday sighed and wondered if she would be able to throw off her feelings for the Baron as easily. She thought not.

The morning proved fine and still warm. They set out after breakfast, Loveday sitting with the Baron because the other two took it for granted that they should share the back seat. To begin with her conversation was a little stilted, but even if she hadn't forgotten the previous evening, her companion appeared to have done so; he was casually friendly and seemingly intent on her enjoyment of the outing, and even if she had wanted to talk about anything other than the pleasant nothings he kept to, she would have been given no opportunity. Presently, lulled by the colourful surroundings and the warm morning, and above all by his friendly manner, she began to enjoy herself; she might just as well; it wouldn't help matters at all by yearning over the impossible and at least she had the consolation of knowing that Rimada was going to be happy – was happy already, judging by the laughter and happy chatter coming from the back seat. Loveday forced her thoughts into more cheerful channels and became very nearly the life and soul of the party.

The sleigh ride was fun; the two girls arrived at the bottom of the hill long before the men with the car. They wandered about, visited the church, bought postcards and souvenirs, and then went and sat in the little village café nearby and ordered coffee. The men joined them presently and the rest of the morning was spent sitting in the sunshine drinking more coffee and talking in a pleasant desultory fashion before Adam drove them back along the coast road and eventually to Funchal and the hotel. A quiet, almost dull morning, but delightful – no rush, no hurry, nothing to do but enjoy themselves. By lunchtime Loveday was nicely relaxed despite her problems.

There wasn't a great many shops in Funchal, although opposite the hotel there was a row of expensive boutiques, flower shops and confectioners. They wandered across to them after their lunch, and Rimada, quite forgetful of the fact that she had no money any more, bought a great many costly trifles and then asked Adam placidly if he would pay for them. Which he did with no word of complaint. Guake bought several things too; Loveday suspected that he was buying them for Rimada because she had admired them. She herself was contented to purchase a scarf which would do very well for her mother and which cost a good deal more than she could afford to spend, and when Adam asked her if she could see anything she liked for herself, she was careful to say no, for fear he might feel called upon to buy things for her too.

They wandered off into the town presently, to explore the pretty gardens and smell the frangipani trees and admire the flowers, and then walked on through the town to the church in its centre. It was dark and cool inside and Loveday wandered off on her own, to find shortly that Rimada and Guake had disappeared and the Baron was waiting patiently for her by the door. He smiled but made no reply to her apology and they went out into the sunshine together, and since there was no sign of the other two, they wandered from shop to shop, stopping for tea at a pavement table outside a café. The Baron had never been so pleasant. Back at the hotel they found Rimada and Guake already there, leaning over the terrace balustrade. They turned surprised faces as they joined them, observing that the afternoon had come and gone so quickly and suggested drinks before they went to change for dinner, and then asked, a little belatedly, if their companions had enjoyed their afternoon too.

Loveday made no answer beyond a polite murmur, leaving it to the Baron to express his opinion, something which he did with conventional politeness and no warmth, confirming her suspicions that he had been merely filling in time in her company so that the others might feel free to go off on their own. Well, possibly she had deserved it, but he could have pretended; she reminded herself that he wasn't a man to pretend. She was being paid back for her disgraceful behaviour of the evening before.

She sipped her drink and wondered if it would be possible to cry off the evening's entertainment with a sick headache. She frowned; possible or not, that was what she intended doing. It would be a pity, of course, because she had planned to wear a particularly charming dress, silk voile, coral pink and most becoming to her, but since the Baron wouldn't even notice it, that didn't matter. She made no mention of her imaginary headache, however, until she and Rimada went to their rooms, when she voiced her uncertainty as to whether she could face the evening in any other place than her bed. They had packed once more, ready for their flight to Lisbon on the following morning, now Rimada was sitting, as usual, at Loveday's dressing table, trying out a variety of hair-styles. She turned and surveyed Loveday with some concern. 'You poor thing – of course you shall go to bed, and it will not matter in the least, for Adam said only this morning that he had his own plans for this evening. I asked him because Guake and I thought we might go for a stroll, but we didn't like to do that until we discovered what you two wanted to do. But now that is most convenient, is it not?'

'Very,' agreed Loveday. Especially for Adam, who must have been wondering how he was going to shake her off so that he could follow his own amusement. She had a bath and got into bed, and when Rimada came back presently to see how she was, remembered to say that the headache was no better, but that a couple of Panadols and a warm drink would soon settle it.

'I'll get someone to send up up some dinner,' offered Rimada, rustling to the telephone. 'What do you fancy?'

Loveday considered. Since she would be forced to spend the evening in bed, she might as well have a good meal to while away the time.

'Iced consommé,' she decided, 'some of those little fish we had last night, and that baked duck with rice was very good – just a water ice will do nicely for afters.'

Rimada conveyed her wishes to the reception desk and added: 'I'll tell them to send you some white wine, shall I? and coffee afterwards. You're sure you're all right?'

Loveday arranged herself more comfortably in her bed. 'Fine,' she said quite cheerfully. 'I'll be perfectly all right here; a good night's sleep and I'll be O.K. – pop in on your way to bed.'

There was a paperback in her case which she hadn't even opened; when Rimada had gone, she hopped out of bed and found it and settled back on her pillows with it opened before her. She read the first page and then let the book fall while she considered her wasted evening. She had never felt better, she had to admit that; being in love must be good for one, even if that love was hopeless. She wondered what the others were doing – having a drink, she supposed; she wondered too if Adam had shown concern when Rimada had told him that she wouldn't be coming down. He was unlikely to care in the very least, reason reminded her; he had his plans for the evening, Rimada had said so. Loveday picked up the book again and read the next few pages with increasing pettishness. She had played right into his hands, hadn't she? Now he could go off and enjoy himself. 'And may it do him good!' she muttered furiously, and had her train of thought interrupted by a knock on the door. She put the book down and called 'Come in'. Dinner would relieve the monotony, at any rate.

It wasn't her dinner, it was Rimada, and hard on her heels Adam, elegant and unhurried, his handsome face infuriatingly calm. He walked over to the bed and stood looking down at Loveday, and it was impossible to tell whether his concern was genuine or not. Probably not.

She eyed him warily while her heart thudded its delight at the sight of him. He said cheerfully: 'Sorry to hear about the headache, I thought I'd better come along and see how you were, though. Perhaps you've had too much sun.' His voice was smooth and professional. 'You were wise to go to bed; I've taken the liberty of cancelling your order for dinner and substituted something more suitable; we can't have you ill.' His eyes fell upon the book. 'I shouldn't read either,' he added, still smooth.

He had whisked the book away as he spoke, keeping it in his hand. 'If I might advise a light supper and then a good sleep. Are you prone to headaches?'

She shook her head; she couldn't remember ever having had one, although she felt reasonably certain that if he went on in the same strain, she would experience one of some magnitude.

'I'm sorry about this evening,' she told him woodenly. 'Luckily you have your own plans made, so Rimada told me.'

She wondered why he should look so amused, although he said nothing, leaving Rimada to fuss round the bed for a minute or two and repeat her promise to come in on her way to bed, before they took their leave.

Loveday fumed. He had taken her book with him, so she had nothing to read; she had done her nails that morning and washed her hair, she had packed, she had, in fact, done everything necessary and time-consuming. She could, of course, take another bath. She was saved the necessity of doing this when there was another tap on the door and a chambermaid came in with her dinner tray. Loveday eyed it anxiously, wondering what the Baron had substituted for her own choice. Bouillon, a small portion of steamed fish with no trimmings, and a miniature jelly were sustained by a few grapes artistically arranged in a small glass dish, the whole flanked by a glass of what she discovered to be tonic water.

She ate the lot very slowly so that it might seem more than it was, wondering the while how she could possibly be head over heels in love with a man who could be so utterly beastly as to starve her – and to take away the only book she had. She drained the last drop of tonic water, got out of bed and went to sit on the balcony in her dressing gown. It was a beautiful evening, but she ignored the moon; it hadn't been of much use the night before, it merely mocked her now. She sat on, thinking of Adam, and when she wasn't thinking of him she was thinking of the splendid breakfast she would eat in the morning. An early swim, she decided, and then a really good meal. Quite cheered by the thought, she went back to bed and much to her surprise, fell asleep so soundly that when Rimada peeped in she didn't stir.

She had the pool to herself the next morning. Fortified by her early tea, she swam its length and back again and then climbed on to the low diving board. She didn't dive well and then only from a foot or two, but as there was no one to see, it was a splendid chance to get some practice. She did rather well, and much emboldened, she climbed higher. She was on the end of the highest diving board when she looked down. The pool looked a long way away, she found herself unable to take her eyes away and the longer she looked the higher she seemed to be. She began to shake with fright while she tried in vain to remember that the pool wasn't far away at all; that she wasn't thousands of feet up. She longed to turn back, but her feet were glued to the board. She went on staring helplessly, feeling sick.

'Just stay there,' Adam's voice from somewhere behind and below her sounded completely reassuring. 'I'm coming up.

'Turn round,' he ordered her, seconds later.

'I can't,' she admitted miserably, 'I shall fall.'

She felt his hands on her shoulders. 'Close your eyes and trust me,' he advised. 'Now turn round.'

Loveday did as she was told and stood shuddering. At his 'Good girl, keep your eyes shut', she nodded and then gave a gasp as she felt his hands relax for a second. He had turned round too, her hands were on his shoulders now, his own holding them there. 'Now walk,' commanded the Baron in a voice which defied disobedience.

Safely on the ground once more, he wasted no time in questions or sympathy. 'Race you to the end of the pool and back,' he said, and pushed her gently in.

It wasn't until they had swum, side by side, for five minutes or so that he said: 'Now a good rub down and breakfast,' and hauled her out as though she had been a rag doll, set her gently on her feet, wrapped her robe around her and trotted her back to the hotel. Only as they parted he remarked matter-of-factly: 'Don't do that again, dear girl,' and then, surprisingly: 'I missed you last night.'

Loveday hugged the robe to her, her eyes on his face. It gave nothing away, as usual. 'You had your evening planned,' she reminded him. 'Rimada . . .'

He smiled. 'Quite right, I had, but Rimada didn't wait to find out if you were included in my plans. You were. Is the headache better?'

She went red. 'Yes, thank you,' she answered him, and sped away to her room.

Breakfast was a carefree meal; Loveday ate hers with appetite and no one mentioned her headache, only as they left the table did Adam say softly to her: 'I daresay you were hungry, Loveday.' A remark she saw fit not to answer.

CHAPTER SEVEN

LOVEDAY hadn't liked the idea of flying to Lisbon, but she had been given no other choice. Everyone flew nowadays, she told herself stoutly as they drove to the airport outside Funchal, and to proclaim her fright at the very idea was to admit to being a coward. She sat, rather white about the mouth, beside the Baron, making conversation while her mouth became more and more dry. They had cleared Customs and were actually going on board when he caught her by the arm. 'I'll sit on the outside,' he told her briefly, and gave her an understanding smile. 'You'll be quite all right, just don't look out until we're airborne – it's not at all the same as looking over the edge of something, you know.'

Rimada and Guake were sitting across the aisle. The Baron squeezed his substantial person past Loveday and sat down, almost obscuring any view Loveday might have had; he also took her hand and held it. He held it for the entire journey – some five hundred and sixty miles, only relinquishing it when refreshments were served and when, having screwed up her courage, she went with Rimada to tidy herself. Back in her seat once more she remarked with relief: 'It's not nearly as bad as I thought it would be.'

He had taken her hand again. 'Good – you won't mind flying on to Amsterdam tomorrow, then.'

'No. I'm sorry to be so silly – it's been boring for you.'

His voice was nicely friendly. 'Not at all. We all have an Achilles heel, you know, only it isn't always discovered.'

'Have you a chink in your armour, too?' she asked.

He turned a faintly smiling face to hers. 'But of course. Will you feel like going out this evening, do you suppose? I expect you and Rimada will want to go shopping before tea – the hotel is near the best of the shops. That will leave us tomorrow morning in which to drive to Sintra and Cascais, there won't be time for more than that, I'm afraid. We can lunch somewhere on the way. Our flight leaves in the late afternoon.'

'You're taking a great deal of trouble. It sounds lovely . . . oh, dear,' she broke off, 'whatever was that?' She clutched at the large hand holding hers so confidently.

'Nothing to worry about; we have to fasten our seat belts now, we're coming in to land. Tomorrow you'll feel much better about flying. You shall look out and I'll point out the interesting things to see – there are a great number.'

Loveday agreed halfheartedly, discovering at the same time that although she hadn't exactly enjoyed the flight, sitting with Adam had been well worth it; she hoped that he would hold her hand again on the morrow's trip.

There was a car waiting for them at the airport; Adam, as Guake explained to Loveday, disliked taxis and preferred to drive himself. She wondered a little at the thought he must have put into the whole trip; the plans which must have been made and then carried out with such apparent lack of effort. She sat beside him once more, driving down the Avenida Almirante Reis towards Lisbon, less than three miles away. The city looked nice; she felt regrets that they wouldn't be staying long enough to see it properly, and when she voiced this thought the Baron said idly: 'Well, we must see what we can do about a next time, mustn't we, Loveday?'

It was one of those remarks which she found so difficult to answer. She mumbled at something and lapsed into silence again, a silence only broken when they arrived at the rather splendid hotel where he had chosen to stay; the Condestavel, close to the Avenida da Liberdade, a thoroughfare which looked to her to be very like the Champs Elysées.

They wasted no time; the girls, after a satisfied inspection of their rooms and half an hour in which to tidy their persons, joined the men in the foyer, and went off to inspect the shops. Not all of them were open, for the midday closing was a lengthy one, but they pored over the enticing goods in the windows and then had an early cup of tea in one of the fashionable tea-shops in the Rua Garrett before pursuing this delightful pastime. They got back to the hotel an hour or so later, Rimada having bought a quantity of lace, some embroidered tablecloths, several silver ornaments she had taken a fancy to, and a small figurine she had been given by Guake. Only her three companions' combined persuasive powers had prevented her from purchasing a set of cane chairs for the garden at home. Loveday had made more modest purchases – some small figures carved from cork, a silver bracelet for Phyllis, a stole for her mother. There was a great deal more that she would have liked to buy, but she wasn't sure yet about returning to England; she had to keep back enough money for her fare.

No one had made any mention of their plans once they got to Holland and she was beginning to wonder if Rimada's mother would be quite as delighted to see her as Adam had made out. In her room, changing into the coral pink dress she hadn't been able to wear in Madeira, she tried to make some plans of her own. Without much success, as it turned out, as Rimada – a transformed Rimada with apparently not a care in the world – came in to have her dress zipped up and stayed talking until Loveday was ready.

The Baron, she saw at once, was in the best of humours – and why not? she thought bitterly, he had had everything his own way – at great expense, no doubt, and with a lot of inconvenience to himself, but everything was turning out exactly as he had planned it should. Rimada, recovering fast from her little affair with Terry Wilde, seemed more than content with Guake. Guake was well on the way to getting what he wanted – Rimada, and the Baron . . . she had no idea what he wanted. Nothing, probably; he had everything. That left herself, with feelings annoyingly mixed; happy to be in the wretched man's company and yet anxious to get away from him before he left a lasting scar on her life.

They dined deliciously and at their leisure, and Loveday found the gaiety of the other three reflecting, dimly perhaps, in herself, and listened in some astonishment to her own voice, as gay as the others. She managed to laugh a great deal too, nicely concealing the awful muddle of thoughts going inside her head.

They toured the city afterwards, stopping for drinks at one of the fashionable cafés and admiring the various buildings which the Baron pointed out to them. At length he parked the car and guided them through the older part of the city – Alfama, and so to the park overlooking the hill they had just climbed, past its medieval houses, the winding roads bringing them finally to the top. Here they walked in the gardens, and made brave by the semi-darkness, Loveday peered cautiously over the ancient battlements, to the distant Tagus and the lights of the city below, quite dimmed by the moonlight. The Baron had put a protecting arm around her as she stood, and when they went slowly back again, it was still there, warm and heavy around her shoulders. He stopped to let the other two go on ahead as they left the park.

'A gorgeous moon,' he observed. 'What is it your poet Yeats wrote? "and pluck till time and times are done the silver apples of the moon." I know now what he meant.'

She didn't answer him and he didn't seem to expect it, only walked on slowly. The old streets were very quiet and just for a little while, there was no time. Loveday hadn't felt as happy in all her life before.

They all met for an early breakfast in the morning. It was a glorious morning with a promise of warmth, though when they started out there was a faint, cool breeze. Loveday, in front with Adam, was surprised to find that he knew exactly where he was going. 'Do you know Portugal well?' she wanted to know.

'Only this locality – I've been here several times, but never for a long period. There's a new teaching hospital here – the Santa Maria . . .'

'You lecture?'

'Yes.' He was driving up the hill, away from the town. 'You like it here?'

So he wasn't going to talk about his work. 'Very much, though I've seen nothing of it, have I? but Lisbon is very pleasant.'

He nodded. 'We're going to Queluz first, there's a summer palace there you might like to see.' And after that he didn't speak until they arrived at the little town. The palace was charming, not large as such places went, perhaps, but its large, single-storey rooms, leading the one into the other, housed some charming furniture, and their guide was equally charming. Too much so, thought Loveday crossly, for the girl had attached herself to the Baron and was chattering away like an old friend, pausing in a conversation which they both obviously found most entertaining, to pass on some interesting piece of information to the rest of the party. Loveday was pleased to see her go once they were in the palace gardens and with the contrariness of a woman in love, at once attached herself to Guake, leaving a slightly put out Rimada to stroll with her cousin.

But it was impossible to stay remote for long. For one thing, the Baron was quite unmoved by her coolness of manner, and for another they were soon at Sintra, a fairylike little town in the mountains, their peaks towered over its great palace, its small square and narrow streets lined with old houses, and each peak was crowned with a castle, ruined for the most part, but adding a picturesque touch which enchanted the two girls. The palace dominated the town, its great arches and steps leading from the square, its quaint chimneys, like Kentish oasthouses, bulging along its face.

They wandered through its rooms, part Gothic, part Moorish, climbed the many stairs and admired the tiled floors, and this time the guide was elderly and walked ahead of them and the Baron kept a light hold on Loveday's arm during the whole of their visit. He was still holding it as they all crossed the square to the hotel opposite, to sit on its terrace and drink their coffee, and when an old woman, in her eye-catching costume, offered them some beautifully dressed dolls, Adam bought one for each of the girls, and then bought two more. 'For your small sister,' he said to Loveday, 'and for your mother, if she would care to accept it.'

He sounded so friendly that she looked at him with suspicion as she thanked him, but there was no mockery in the look he gave her, only a placid friendliness. Perhaps, she thought hopefully, they were no longer on opposite sides. Perhaps the dolls were an olive branch? Certainly they were delightful souvenirs and Phyllis and her mother would love them. She still had to explain to her family about the different arrangements which had been made; it had been impossible to say anything on the postcards she had sent – upon reflection, it seemed a good idea to wait until she got home; a letter would be difficult; besides, there would be no opportunity to get it written before they left for Amsterdam. She dismissed the little worry from her mind and, pressed by Rimada, had another cup of coffee.

They left Sintra by the winding hilly road leading to the sea, lined at its beginning with large villas set in colourful gardens, which presently petered out into a rather wild and beautiful countryside, with the rocky mountains still towering at a distance. It would have been nice to have had more time to explore, but as the Baron pointed out, they needed to be back in Lisbon by half past three at the latest, and although they weren't far from the city, there was a good deal of interest to see before they reached it.

They were at Cascais a few minutes later, an enchanting little town by the sea where the Baron had planned lunch. There was a tremendous amount to see. Leaving Rimada to go off happily with Guake, Adam whisked Loveday to the fish market and then to the beach where the fishing boats were drawn up, and from there to a charming park before allowing her a lightning glimpse of the shops. She had barely begun to study their contents when he walked her briskly to the Casas Hotel, listening good-humouredly to her annoyed comments on being rushed away from some of the most interesting shops she had seen.

'Another time,' was all he would say to console her, and grinned when she protested: 'But I daresay I'll never come here again – all those lovely embroidered head-scarves . . .'

'Which ones were they?' he asked lazily.

'Those appliquéd ones,' she told him, quite carried away by the thought of them. 'Oh, there are Guake and Rimada, how pleased they look with themselves.'

'Naturally,' he sounded smug.

They had a hilarious lunch, eating the local specialities; *gazpacho*, a cold soup of bread and onions and garlic, oil and vinegar and coriander seeds, and the *lulas guizadas*, which Loveday didn't discover was octopus until she had eaten, and enjoyed, it. They finished with *arroz doce* which turned out to be a glorified rice pudding with cinnamon, and they washed these local dainties down with a Madeira wine carefully chosen by their host.

Estoril, after that, seemed but a pale reflection of Cascais. Pretty enough, clean and white and bright with colour in the sunshine, and richly full of large villas, but the gardens before its casino weren't as pretty as the little park in Cascais, and the sea-front, delightful though it was, lacked the character of the other little town. All the same, Loveday made herself a promise to come again one day while she listened to Rimada's plans for another, longer holiday in Portugal next year. They were very definite plans, she noted, and Guake agreed with all of them.

It was nice to see her friend so happy, but she felt a little sad too; she would miss her at the Royal City, although she had plenty of other friends. She supposed that in time she would slip back into her old way of life; the jaunts to the cinema and theatre, the shopping on pay day, the occasional dinner with some houseman or other, but very soon she would be getting a little old for housemen, and in any case, if she couldn't go out to dinner with Adam, she wasn't sure that she cared about going out with anyone else. The future looked a little dim.

Back in the hotel there was just time for a cup of tea before they dispersed to their rooms to prepare for the journey to Amsterdam. Loveday packed, wondering about excess baggage, making uneasy calculations as to its cost – something which Rimada, when asked, dismissed as a trifle which Adam would see to. Loveday changed into a cotton jersey dress in a pleasing shade of mushroom and caught up its matching jacket; she was a bit vague about such things, but presumably it would be a good deal cooler in Holland. It was, after all, early October.

The porter came for their luggage and at the same time handed her a small package, wrapped in the expensive paper found only in the best boutiques.

'There's a mistake,' she said positively. 'The other young lady . . .'

The man shook his head. 'For you, miss,' and slid away with her cases before she could stop him. She turned the package over, examining it from all sides. There was no name on it, nothing to say for whom it was or from who it had been sent. She opened it slowly. There were two scarves inside, of a deep rose pink and a moss green of great delicacy; they were of silk and beautifully embroidered with the appliqué work she had admired in Cascais. Between them, on a leaf of paper torn from a pocket book and in Adam's writing, were the words: 'A small memento of a pleasant day.' It was signed simply, 'Adam.'

She touched them with a gentle finger. He had gone away after lunch, she remembered, he must have bought them then; a kindly act, especially when she considered the stormy path of their acquaintance. She folded them carefully and put them in her overnight bag. Later on, when she was back in London, she would wear them and remember him each time she did so; not that she would need anything to remind her of him. She took a last quick look at her reflection in the mirror and wondered at the calm face staring back at her, while inside her, her heart was sick at the very thought of not seeing him again once they got back to Holland. She kept that outward calm when they went downstairs to find the two men and while she thanked Adam for his gift.

He heard her out, smiling a little. 'I felt guilty,' he told her. 'Let's say that they are merely a salving of my conscience.' A remark which turned her rather melancholy train of thought to instant pique, so that her manner became brightly brittle and her conversation stilted to say the least. The Baron, driving them all to the airport, let her rattle on, making monosyllablic replies and then only when necessary. She was so busy talking to mask her feelings that she quite failed to notice that he was deep in thought. Those same feelings were so strong, that she hardly realized that they had gone through Customs and had boarded the plane – indeed, they buoyed her up during the take-off and when the Baron asked her if she felt able to admire the view she told him quite tartly that she saw no reason why she shouldn't, whereupon he leaned back in his seat so that she might look at the panorama of Lisbon and the Tagus, and in the distance, the great bridge spanning it, quite failing to notice the smile tugging at the corners of his mouth and the gleam in his eyes. When she at length sat back beside him, he observed mildly: 'I see that you are cured.'

She quite forgot that her feelings were upset. 'I wasn't thinking about it,' she confessed.

'So I imagined. All the same, I shouldn't go dangling over cliff tops or looking over high walls. Being in an aeroplane isn't quite the same thing.'

She agreed meekly enough, accepted the sweet and magazine the air hostess was offering her, and settled down quietly to read, because her companion had taken some papers out of his brief case and was obviously intent on studying them and she was as capable of taking a hint as the next one, and because she was a little tired and the sight of him sitting there reading, just as though he were at home with his feet on his own hearthrug, lulled her to security, she closed her eyes and slept. She didn't wake until the three-hour flight was almost over, a fact which she was thankful, for she felt faintly queasy. She sat very still, hoping the awful feeling would pass – perhaps if she thought of something else, to concentrate was the thing.

Her companion's voice precluded any such thing. 'Feeling sick?' he asked, not mincing matters. 'Have some of this.' He put a brandy flask into her hand, adding encouragingly: 'Drink up!'

Loveday drank, said 'Ugh!' and at his insistence, drank again. The brandy burnt her mouth and throat and brought tears to her eyes, it also made her feel very much better. The Baron removed the flask from her grasp and put it back in his hip pocket.

'We'll be down in five minutes,' he assured her. 'Do you want to powder your nose?'

Fortified by the brandy and with Rimada in support, Loveday went to tidy herself, carefully not looking out of any windows, and although she said nothing at all when she got back to her seat, the Baron strapped her in in a kindly fashion and took her hand once more in his large, comforting grasp.

Normally, she might have given some thought as to what came next after they arrived at Schipol, but even a few days in the Baron's company had accustomed her to effortless travel with all the snags nicely ironed out; it didn't surprise her in the least to find his Rolls waiting for them. There was an elderly man at the wheel whom she recognized as Sieska's husband. He got out as they approached, exchanged greetings, stowed the luggage and then stood waiting patiently while Adam and Guake had a short conference. Adam came back after a few minutes, saying by way of explanation: 'Guake's car is here; he'll drive Rimada and I'll drop you off at

Wassenaar as we go. In with you.' He nodded to the elderly man, who got into the back.

There seemed no choice, and even if she could have made one, she would have chosen to go with him. Every minute of his company counted now; once he had returned to the fastness of his home in Friesland, she wasn't likely to see him before she returned to England. There was still a few days of her holiday left and she wasn't quite happy at the idea of being foisted on to Freule de Wolff with no warning whatsoever. She ventured to give voice to her doubts as the Baron sent the car speeding along the motorway.

'Dear girl, how you fuss – my aunt will be delighted to welcome you.'

She shot him an exasperated look. 'How do you know? And how are you going to explain about Rimada losing all her money?'

She saw his mouth curve in a smile. 'She will be more than satisfied at the outcome of the whole miserable affair – for one thing, she had always fancied Guake as a son-in-law, and for another it has cost her nothing at all other than that quite unnecessary sum of money she gave Rimada.'

'Perhaps she will think I am to blame? for helping Rimmy, I mean.'

'Probably.' His voice was disinterested and she looked away, out of the window. He knew everything. No, not everything; he didn't know how much she loved him, but wild horses wouldn't drag that from her. Sitting quietly beside him, answering his idle remarks suitably, she began to think about her future; Rimada wasn't going back with her, though presumably she would have to return to hospital at some future date to see Matron. Presumably, too, she herself could make her own plans to leave in a couple of days or so, and surely Rimada's mother would be glad if she did. She wondered about Guake – was he going to stay too? She wasn't sure where he lived – somewhere in Friesland, she believed, but no doubt he would want to remain and consolidate his position with Rimada, so to speak. She became aware that her companion was speaking and had no idea what he had said. 'I'm sorry,' she uttered, a little flustered, 'I didn't hear . . .'

'Daydreams,' he murmured, 'or are you plotting something in that pretty head?' He glanced at her sharply. 'Don't tell me that you disapprove of Guake?'

'Guake? Of course not, he's just right for Rimmy, really he is; he's so kind, and he'll take such care of her, as long as she's sure this time.'

He allowed the car to ooze past a bunch of slow-moving traffic.

'The exact antithesis of me,' he observed cheerfully. 'And don't worry about her being sure, he'll take care of that.' His voice changed to one of faint mockery. 'So you feel that being taken care of and treated kindly are essentials of a happy marriage?'

'But of course they are,' said Loveday in an astonished voice, knowing even as she said it that personally, she wouldn't care about either of those attributes. Just to be loved, as long as it was Adam who loved her, would do very nicely. She sighed and he gave a short laugh.

'My poor girl, can't you tell your dreams from reality yet? Escape from moonshine, Loveday.'

And wasn't that exactly what she was trying to do, for was he not himself moonshine in her life? A pity she couldn't tell him that, she mused bitterly, and sighed again.

'Do you start work tomorrow?' she asked him woodenly, and was put out at his laugh.

'Snubbed,' he told her cheerfully. 'You're in a nasty frame of mind, aren't you? Yes, I'll start tomorrow. Thanks to Rimada – and you – I've a backlog of cases which will take me a couple of weeks' hard work to clear.'

An unfair remark which did nothing to douse her cross feelings, but she hadn't the spirit to cross swords with him, instead she began a stilted conversation about the merits of a temperate climate, a singularly inept subject, seeing that it had begun to rain from a grey, dreary evening sky.

Her vague doubts about her welcome took a concrete form when they arrived at Rimada's home. The first excited interlocutions over, and an invitation to remain and eat supper having been refused by the two men, Freule de Wolff turned to Loveday.

'And you, Loveday,' she wanted to know, 'no doubt you have your plans made to return to England as soon as possible.' She smiled without warmth. 'But of course, you must stay the night here; we can arrange for you to be taken to Schiphol as early as you wish in the morning.'

Loveday blinked and shot a look at the Baron. It was an 'I told you so' look, which he received with a bland expression which infuriated her.

'You won't mind if we speak Dutch?' was all he said to her, and without waiting for her reply, addressed his aunt. His voice sounded placid, firm, and very quiet, but it produced a flood of tears on the part of his aunt as well as a chokingly angry retort.

'My aunt is under some misapprehension,' he explained smoothly. 'She seems to think that it was your bad influence which caused Rimada to embark upon her disastrous affair with young Wilde.'

Loveday made an impatient sound. 'Well, really – do explain, will you?'

'I have, but with no good result, I'm afraid – you see, it is very difficult for me to deny that you helped Rimada in every way possible. However,' he went on, still smooth, 'I have persuaded her to invite you to stay for a few days. Guake will be coming tomorrow evening. I'm sure Rimada will be glad of your company.'

Loveday fumed silently, and although her lovely face looked calm, her eyes held a dangerous sparkle. She said, very low: 'So we're on opposite sides once more – I thought . . .' She swallowed and began again, this time speaking to her unwilling hostess. 'I'm sorry if you think that I encouraged Rimada. Perhaps I did. I don't know any more, and anyway, what would be the use . . .' she interrupted herself to say to the impassive man watching her, 'but I do remember why I got involved, and that was your fault, Professor de Wolff.' She turned her back on him then and addressed herself to Freule de Wolff.

'Of course you don't want me here as a guest, since you think so badly of me. If I may stay the night and leave tomorrow, as soon after breakfast as you can arrange it.' And at an impatient sound from the Baron she turned round. 'You can be quiet,' she told him sharply. 'I'm very glad to be saying good-bye to you, although you have such a good opinion of yourself that I daresay you won't believe me.'

She nodded at him and crossed the room to where Rimada and Guake, deep in their own conversation, hadn't heard a word.

'Rimmy,' she said, breaking ruthlessly into their conversation, 'your mother had been awfully kind and asked me to stay, but I've decided to go tomorrow. You won't mind awfully, will you? It's been great fun, hasn't it?' she stumbled over the lie, 'but if you're not coming back to the Royal City, then I'll go home for a couple of days, get my clothes sorted out and so on.' She smiled at her friend. The dear girl looked so happy, perhaps at last she knew what she wanted, and now was no time in which to beg her to clear up the misunderstanding her mother was labouring under.

Rimada looked mildly surprised. 'Loveday, must you? I planned to do some shopping – only a little because I haven't any money, but it would have been fun. Still, I daresay Mama will come with me.' She added anxiously: 'You aren't peeved? I mean, it wasn't quite what we had planned.' She glanced up at Guake, standing placidly silent beside them. 'You'll come over when you have a few days? I shall miss hospital life.'

'Not for long,' said Guake quietly, and they smiled at each other so that Loveday felt very lonely.

'I've a raging headache,' she said. 'Would you mind if I went straight to bed?'

'But supper?'

'I'm not hungry. Would your mother excuse me?'

Rimada called something to her mother across the room and then said:

'Mother says there is a room ready, the one you had last time, and if there's anything you want, you have only to ring. You're sure, Loveday?'

'Yes, thanks, Rimmy.' She wished them both good night and crossed the room once more and bade her hostess good night too, but to Adam she nodded briefly without a word as she passed him. But he was too quick for her; he was at the door before she could reach it.

'A pity,' he said quietly. 'I wanted to talk to you – to explain; I've changed my mind. I'm staying for supper after all.'

She raised her eyebrows and gave him a stony stare, willing herself not to burst into tears. 'A pity – I'm going to bed, it seems the best thing to do in the circumstances. Besides, I have a headache.'

His blue eyes searched hers. 'I'll allow you your mythical headache,' he told her slowly. 'You're upset, but I shall be back tomorrow morning, we'll have our talk then.'

She had nothing to say, she went past him through the door he was holding for her and upstairs without looking back. In her room she undressed and bathed rapidly, unpacked a jersey trouser suit, repacked her

146

case and counted her money. She had more than sufficient, she was pleased to discover, for the hare-brained scheme she had in mind. She set her little alarm clock for four o'clock in the morning and got into bed, carefully going over her plan to make sure that it was a good one. She went to sleep in the middle of its rehearsal.

Her room was at the end of a passage at the back of the house, while Rimada's and her mother's were at the front. The alarm made little noise, she thought it unlikely that anyone would have heard it. She dressed and a little hampered by her case and overnight bag, crept down the stairs.

It was dark and decidedly chilly, and a cup of coffee would have been just the thing, but she didn't dare try to find the kitchen. The front door was bolted and barred, but its hinges and bolts were well oiled. Loveday left the notes she had written to Rimada and her mother on the hall table and set to work to open the door. A few minutes more and she was outside, walking stealthily towards the gate and thankful to find that it was open. It was getting on for five o'clock and starting to drizzle with rain. She knew that it was two miles to Wassenaar and another five to The Hague; with luck she might find someone to give her a lift from Wassenaar; there might even be an early morning bus. She set out along the road Adam had so recently taken with the car, her mind resolutely empty of any thoughts other than those concerned with getting her home as quickly as possible.

The sky lightened slowly. By the time she had

reached Wassenaar and found a bus stop, there was daylight of sorts, the drizzle had stopped and had given way to a watery sun and a bitter little wind; Loveday felt thankful for the trouser suit as she took her place at the end of the bus queue.

It was still early when she reached The Hague, but there were a good many people about. She got a taxi without much difficulty and once at the station was thankful to find a small café open where she spent her last few Dutch coins on a cup of coffee. There were trains in plenty going to Amsterdam, and because she had no idea how else to go, she persuaded the clerk to take English money for a ticket, and got on the next train. Her case was a nightmare by now and she seemed to have been travelling for ever; it was with a sigh of relief that she hailed a taxi outside the Centrale Station in Amsterdam and asked to be taken to Schiphol.

Once there she inquired, a little anxiously, about a flight to London, to be told that yes, there would be one in half an hour and she could have a seat on it. Loveday paid with her fast diminishing money, reflecting that she had had luck on her side so far, handed over her cases and went to join the little knot of people waiting for her flight. It was still not yet nine o'clock. Rimada and her mother seemed miles away, in another world already – Adam's world, but not hers. She swallowed tears as she boarded the plane.

CHAPTER EIGHT

THE flight was a bumpy one. Loveday sat with her eyes closed, swallowing fright, wanting the feel of Adam's hand on hers, very badly. Half-way across the Channel, she fell asleep and awoke, to her intense relief in time to hear the hostess uttering the welcome warning to fasten her seat belt.

She went straight to the hospital, organized her clothes, got out the Morris and without seeing anyone at all, drove herself home. Her mother was alone; Phyllis was at school, her father playing golf, and if Mrs. Pearce found it surprising to see her elder daughter walk into the house three days before she was due back from her cruise, she concealed it very well, merely remarking that she was delighted to see her; that she had thought that the cruise lasted longer but that she must have been mistaken and expressed the hope that Loveday was going to be home for a few days. Loveday hugged her, grateful for her lack of curiosity and the masterly control which prevented her from asking questions.

'Things turned out rather differently from what we had expected,' began Loveday cautiously. 'I'll tell you while we have a cup of coffee.'

Sitting cosily at the kitchen table, her mother remarked matter-of-factly: 'You must have left in the early hours of the morning, darling, I do hope you haven't been travelling all the time – and what about breakfast?'

Loveday skated over these leading questions with a few mutters and began carefully, choosing her words. 'You see, Rimada wanted to come home sooner than we intended – someone she's known for ages – such a nice man, was waiting at Madeira when we arrived there and of course Rimmy decided to come back with him. There wasn't much point in my going on alone ... we got back yesterday and although Rimmy's mother asked me to stay, I thought I'd like to come home for the last few days. You don't mind?'

Something in her voice made her mother look thoughtfully at her, but beyond voicing a satisfying enthusiasm at the prospect of Loveday being home, even if only for a day or two, she kept silent. Her daughter's story had been the bare bones of the matter; that would have been obvious to any woman listening to it, but if the dear child didn't want to talk about it, that was her business. 'Only,' thought Mrs. Pearce uneasily, 'I wish she didn't look so unhappy. Some man, of course.' She poured second cups and began to ask questions about the cruise.

It was inevitable that sooner or later the Baron was mentioned, and inevitable too that Mrs. Pearce should ask, in the most casual way possible, if Loveday like him.

'He's very nice. He's a good surgeon, quite well known internationally.'

'Oldish, I daresay,' mused Mrs. Pearce cunningly. 'after all, he is Rimada's guardian.'

'Oh, no, he's only in his late thirties, he's . . .' Loveday perceived her parent's trap and changed her words. 'He's a very busy man, I believe.'

'Oh, yes, I see,' said her mother, who didn't see at all, only that this was undoubtedly the man her dear daughter was unhappy about. Foreigners – she frowned and then smoothed her face into its usual calm.

'I'm glad you're home, darling. I saw a rather nice suit in Tenterden – that boutique on the left going down the hill, I always forget its name. Your father's no help at all and Phyllis is so modern, bless her. We might run down later on and have a look at it.'

Loveday's nerves, at twanging point, relaxed under the placid peace and quiet of home; by the time her father got back after tea, she was laughing and talking away, almost, but not quite, her usual self.

She went back to the Royal City two days later, full of good resolutions about forgetting Adam, throwing herself into her work, and concentrating upon the future. But there was no need for her to make any resolutions about her work; the surgeons' lists were endless, it was like getting a quart into a pint pot. She spent half an hour with the registrars, pointing this fact out to them in a quite ruthless manner, and cutting the lists down to manageable size. Even so, they would all be grossly overworked for the next few weeks.

But she quite welcomed this state of affairs, for it would help her enormously in keeping the second of her resolutions – to forget Adam. Indeed, she succeeded very well with this while she was in theatre, hard at work, but off duty her thoughts tended to harp endlessly upon him, and this despite the fact that she was thinking seriously about her future, although that same future held nothing to interest her, only an endless vista of years, if not at the Royal City, then at some other hospital. Common sense told her that the likelihood of her receiving several offers of marriage before this occurred was more than possible, but she was in no mood to listen to common sense. As far as she was concerned, there were no other men in the world, only Adam.

She had been back a little over a week when Mr. Gore-Symes waylaid her as she was going off duty and begged her in his gentlemanly tones to tart the place up a bit the following morning. 'And before you ask why,' he added a trifle testily, 'let me tell you that there'll be a posse of surgical talent touring the place; don't be surprised if they come trooping into the place once the list has started.'

'To watch that adrenalectomy?' she nodded. 'O.K., sir, but if they dare to come into my theatre not properly gowned and masked, I'll throw the lot of them out, talent or no talent!'

He twinkled at her. 'I'll give them good warning, Loveday.' He started away from her and then paused to ask: 'You're feeling all right? You've looked a bit under the weather since you came back from your holiday.'

She answered briefly: 'I'm quite all right, thank you, sir – a bit tired, I expect – we've been rather pushed, haven't we?'

He nodded as he went, thinking that it wasn't like Loveday Pearce to complain, even mildly, about the amount of extra work she was expected to do. He had known times when they had worked twice as hard and never a word from her.

There were several other cases besides the adrenalectomy; they would be at it all day, Loveday calculated. She was off duty that evening, but the first case would take a great deal longer if a parcel of learned gentlemen were going to argue over it, so she might as well resign herself to a snatched hour before supper. A good thing really, she reminded herself; she had had several long letters from Rimada, full of instructions as to what she should do with her possessions still in her room, descriptions of the new clothes she had bought, and – did her dear Loveday know already? She wasn't penniless after all, not that it mattered because Guake had more than enough of his own. There was a great deal about Guake; orange blossom was definitely in the air.

And Terry Wilde – he had come back to the hospital before she had, and had gone again on some family matter or other. Now he was back once more; Loveday had bumped into him the evening before on her way over to the home and he had been embarrassingly friendly and had asked her with a knowing little smile if she had changed her mind. 'Remember I'm here, Loveday,' he reminded her, and went jauntily on his way, leaving her speechless.

She hadn't slept very well as a consequence of this meeting and went on duty in a frame of mind hardly calculated to view a theatre full of strange men with equanimity. But her spirits took an upward lift at the sight of the gleaming brass and the shining glass as she entered the theatre unit. There were flowers on her desk too, a little touch for which she had no doubt she had Staff to thank. She checked each room in turn; the sterilizing room where only emergency sterilizing was done, the sluice, the anaesthetic room, the tiny kitchen, the surgeons' dressing room, the nurses' cubbyhole, where they crammed their cloaks and handbags and shoes, and then went back to the office. The whole place was in apple pie order, and she only hoped that the posse would notice it; they wouldn't of course, they would bumble in, crowd round the table, getting horribly in the way, and when they had seen enough, they would mutter vaguely in her direction by way of farewell and bumble out again. Men! thought Loveday savagely, vexed with them all and loving one to distraction.

She was arranging the Mayo's table, decking it to her satisfaction and laying out instruments with care upon it, when Mr. Gore-Symes came in, wished her good morning, eyed her without further speech and went out again; she went on with her careful work, supposing him to have forgotten something – he would be back presently; the patient had been wheeled in and arranged just so by the theatre orderlies and Mrs. Thripps. Loveday swept her team together with a lift of the eyebrows and bent to test a pair of Spencer Wells forceps which didn't seem to be up to her high standard. When she looked up, Mr. Gore-Symes was coming into the theatre. He had Gordon Blair with him, the usual two housemen, and towering over them all, Adam.

Loveday regrettably dropped the forceps, quite carried away by a desire to push the trolleys away and fling herself at him; a foolish action fortunately prevented by her years of training. But she did allow herself a reproachful glance at Mr. Gore-Symes, who, even behind his mask, looked sheepish.

It was Adam who broke the silence with a cheerful 'Good morning, Loveday,' and followed this up with an equally cheerful greeting to everyone else standing around. He then engaged Mr. Gore-Symes in a few technicalities, took the scalpel Loveday was offering, and began his work. He didn't speak to her, unless it was to make a request for some instrument or other, for the rest of the operation, there was little opportunity, anyway, for presently a group of gowned and masked figures joined them, and any further remarks he made, were addressed to them.

At the end of the case they stopped for coffee, but not, us usual, in her office. There were far too many of them for that; the gentlemen were accommodated in their dressing room with a large tray loaded with mugs and jugs and sugar bowls, and Loveday, drinking her own coffee with Staff for company, could hear their cheerful voices and occasional bellows of laughter.

'I say,' observed Peggy, 'that was a bit of a surprise, sister – Professor what's-his-name coming in like that. You didn't expect him, did you?'

'No,' said Loveday, and sought frantically for something to say. 'Mr. Gore-Symes did tell me that there would be an audience, but you knew that too, didn't you? I suppose he came over at the last minute and no one remembered to let us know.'

'Well, someone must have known,' pointed out her right hand, 'for his instruments were ready, weren't they?'

Loveday frowned. 'Yes, I know. Oh, well, it doesn't matter, does it? I expect he'll be leaving now with the rest of them.'

But he did no such thing; he assisted Mr. Gore-Symes for the remainder of the morning, and after their midday break, there he was again, bending his height tirelessly over the table. Loveday, who had had to go to her own meal and return early from it, thought crossly that he might consider others occasionally. As the day wore on, her staff came and went, but inevitably towards evening, the group around the table became depleted. Staff had gone off duty at one o'clock, the indefatigible Mrs. Thripps went at half past three, and one student nurse had gone after her dinner; any moment now the faithful Bert, nudged by an invisible union, would down tools. She heaved a sigh, unaware that she had done so, and Adam said quietly: 'Another ten minutes or so, Sister – it's been a long day.'

He looked across at Mr. Gore-Symes, who was removing an appendix with an apparently effortless skill, although he must have been tired too. He threw the offending portion of his patient's anatomy at the kidney dish held out by a nurse and said: 'It's a funny thing, the more we do the more we get, if you see what I mean.' He tied the purse string carefully and Adam snipped the ends for him. 'A good thing you said you would stay, de Wolff – I'm obliged to you. Blair always seems to have a half day when we're extra busy.' He did some neat needlework, pulled off his gloves, stopped to pass the time of day with the anaesthetist, and walked away, followed by Adam.

It took a long time to clear theatre; there were only three of them left by now, and they flagged a little. At last they were ready and Loveday sent the other two off and after ten minutes' work in her office, closed the doors thankfully behind her. It had been a busy day and she was tired; and although it was still early evening, she was already planning an early night. She would skip supper; she had biscuits in her room and she could make a pot of tea, have a long, long bath and go to bed with an armful of magazines.

She dwelt deliberately on these rather dull plans, thrusting to the back of her mind any foolish ideas she might have concerning Adam. He had gone from theatre without a word, and after all, what else could she have expected?

She crossed the entrance hall and made for the little door at the back which would bring her to the inner courtyard and eventually, the Nurses' Home. She was half-way there when she was hailed by Nancy, her red-haired friend from the Accident Room, in a fiery mood to suit her hair, for she began without preamble: 'That wretched woman – she said she would be back before four, and here it is six o'clock and no sign of her – she was off duty at half past, too.'

Loveday came to a halt. 'Trouble?' she inquired, glad to have her unhappy thoughts distracted.

Nancy snorted. 'I'd say – an old lady – brought in this morning with the usual – fell over, Colles' fracture and a bit of a shaking. We put a plaster on and sent her home – she lives nearby in Summer Street – and when she'd gone we found her purse and the dope Teddy gave her for the pain. No one came back for them and Dolly' – Dolly was the department maid – 'said she'd fetch them before she went home and deliver them on her way – now the wretch has gone.' She jerked her brilliant head in the direction of the porter's lodge. 'I've just asked. Now I'll have to take the wretched things. George will just have to wait.'

Loveday knew all about George, Nancy's devoted fiancé. 'Here,' she offered, 'let me have them. I'm off late myself and I've no plans to do anything and it's only five minutes' walk.'

Nancy's face brightened. 'You're a pet – will you really? Number twenty – one of those grotty little houses half way down.'

Loveday had her cloak with her; she shrugged it round her shoulders and made for the entrance, calling a cheerful word or so to Bob, the porter on duty. It was already dusk, but dry; she stepped out briskly, glad of something to do, even if only for half an hour. Summer Street was small and dreary, lined on one side by ugly Victorian houses, grey with smoke and grime, paint-work peeling and windows tight shut, Loveday, who was used to the shabbiness of the neighbourhood, hardly noticed them. Number twenty was a little over half way down the row, opposite a narrow, high-walled alley and the blank wall of some disused warehouse. The air smelled stale and damp, and Loveday wondered how anyone could bear to live there and pitied the occupants of the horrid little houses with all her heart.

It took a long time before anyone answered her knock; she could hear bolts being drawn before at length it was opened cautiously to show an old lady's face.

'It's all right,' said Loveday reassuringly, 'it's someone from the hospital – you left your purse and tablets and I've brought them for you.'

The door was opened wider. 'You'll come in?' said the old lady, and Loveday could hear the eagerness in the old voice. She hadn't meant to stop, but ten minutes would make no difference to her evening and the poor soul was probably lonely. She found herself in a narrow lobby which opened into a small dark room, and it was cold as well as dark. Ushered to a worn-out armchair, she sat down at her companion's bidding and when the old lady asked: 'Yer'll 'ave a cuppa, won't yer, Sister?' she hadn't the heart to refuse; besides, the kettle was already on the gas ring by the empty fireplace.

She sipped the too strong tea from a cup not quite clean, and listened, her kind heart wrung, while the old lady talked. Not that she complained or grumbled; Loveday saw that she was lonely and desperate for company; she sat back in the wreck of a chair and prepared to spend part at least of her evening there. There was little need to say much once her hostess had started; she poured out a miscellany of family history, local gossip and comments on life in general. An old woman of spirit and a good deal of courage, Loveday considered, who had refused help despite her arm in plaster and her bruises and was delighted to play hostess for an hour or so.

It was considerably more than an hour later when she got to her feet. The evening was dark now and she guessed that the old woman would go to bed in order to save lighting a lamp. She bade her a friendly good night, and resolved silently to do something to help – a visit now and then, papers to read, sweets, the odd packet of tea. She started back along the dark little street, making a mental list of suitable things to take. She had gone perhaps twenty yards when a slight sound made her look behind her; there were three figures in the gloom behind her; teenagers, she thought; a girl and two boys. They looked vaguely menacing, but not being of a timid nature, she walked on; the street was silent and empty, but its end wasn't far away and there would be plenty of people around once she gained the main road. She was surprised when the girl ran ahead and then stopped in front of her; she wished her a good evening in a level voice and walked on, but the girl got in her way. Short of running herself, it would be difficult to get away from her, and the two boys were crowding close behind now. Loveday turned to face them.

'If you're thinking of mugging me, you can think

again,' she told them roundly, and quaked inwardly as she spoke. 'I haven't a penny on me, so get on home, do!'

The three of them were encircling her now, moving all the time, saying nothing at all, which was somehow more frightening than anything else. The girl put a hand on her cloak and she shook it off, and when one of the boys caught her other arm she pushed him away so that he almost lost his balance. She was really frightened now, although she knew that if she could keep walking she would shortly reach the main road. She started to walk again saying: 'Don't be so silly, you're not frightening me in the least, and if this is your idea of a joke, then you can stop it!' The girl clutched at her cloak again and she pushed her hard, by now angry as well as frightened. The girl fell over, scrambled to her feet and made for Loveday, intent on revenge. But she didn't get far. From the dark street ahead a hand clamped her firm and then set her on one side, and Adam, stepping silently into the miserable light of the street lamp, caught the two boys in an iron grip, shook them hard and gave them a push. Without bothering to see the results of this exercise, he caught Loveday by the arm, turned his back upon the discomfited three, and began to walk her up the street. His 'Hullo, dear girl,' was almost placid. 'They told me where you might be. No hurt, I trust?'

She was swallowing tears. After a minute she managed. 'No, thank you,' and because that sounded inadequate, she added: 'I was frightened.'

He stopped and turned her to face him under the

light of the next street lamp. The three youngsters had followed them and they stopped too. He looked round at them and said impatiently: 'Get home, the lot of you, and if you try your silly tricks again, I swear I'll come after you and turn you into mincemeat!'

He turned his back on them again and Loveday, unable to help herself, whispered: 'Oh, Adam, be careful!'

He stared down at her without speaking. Presently, after a silence which seemed to last for ever, he said: 'Well, well,' and bent to kiss her, very gently, on the cheek.

But his voice held nothing but friendly cheerfulness as he marched her along once more. 'Dinner, I thought – we never had our little chat, did we? Tell me, just how did you get to Schiphol from my aunt's house? Your letters were a bit vague about that, as were your reasons for going home. I can quite understand that you were put out at my aunt's manner towards you, but put yourself in her place, dear girl . . . she had every reason to be suspicious of you.'

'And you could have stopped her,' said Loveday quite fiercely.

'Yes, so I could, but it wouldn't have done to have set my aunt against her only child, would it? As it is, she considers her to be an innocent girl persuaded into foolhardiness – by you, I'm afraid – and now luckily restored to the maternal bosom until such time as Guake proposes.'

'You had it all worked out . . .' Somehow the knowledge that he had used her quite ruthlessly to gain his own ends, hurt more than anything else. But of course, to him, she had just been an annoying stumbling block in his schemes.

They were almost at the hospital. At its door she said quietly:

'Thanks for bringing me back, and rescuing me, I'm very grateful. Will you give my love to Rimada when you see her?'

She whisked through the door and made off across the entrance hall, her determination badly cracked by the rebel wish that he would come rushing after her. Only he didn't. She reached the door and went through it, not looking back. The courtyard was chilly and half dark and as cheerless as her mood; it had the immediate effect of causing her to burst into silent tears. It took her several minutes to stop crying, out there in the dark, but presently she mopped her face and rushed into the home, not caring in the least what she looked like; everyone would be at supper, anyway.

The Baron was waiting for her, standing at the foot of the stairs, his vast person leaning against its utilitarian banisters. He appeared half asleep, but the eyes beneath their drooping lids were very intent.

'Ah, there you are,' he said easily. 'Now do go and get dressed, there's a good girl – I'm famished. Would you like me to come up and chat while you change?'

Loveday gaped at him. 'How ...' she began, and then: 'Of course you can't come upstairs – it's not allowed.' She had passed him and was on her way up, and he had made no attempt to stop her. 'I don't want to come out with you, thank you.'

He waited until she was right at the top. 'No, I was afraid you wouldn't, but Rimada and Guake are over here with me. Rimada told me that she would never speak to me again if I didn't bring you back with me – hardly a threat I would lose any sleep over! It was to have been a surprise, but I have been forced to tell you, haven't I?'

She had whirled round on the top stair. 'Rimmy here? Where?'

'I said we would meet them at the Brompton Grill.' He glanced at his watch. 'You have ten minutes, Loveday.' He smiled engagingly at her. 'That's if you intend coming ... Rimtsje will be very disappointed if you don't.'

'Why didn't you say so in the first place?' she asked with a decided snap.

He contrived to look humble. 'I had nourished the hope that you might have liked to come, thinking that we would have been on our own.'

To answer him would be to involve herself in a number of pitfalls. 'Wait there,' she begged him, and flew to her room. She was used to changing in a hurry, she had had a shower, got into a fine wool dress and its matching green coat, put up her hair, done her face, found shoes, gloves and handbag, remembered her cherished bottle of 'Femme' and found herself ready in exactly fifteen minutes. If her face was pale, as her reflection showed her, and her eyes were a trifle pink-rimmed, there was nothing to do about that; after all, she had had a nasty shock not half an hour earlier. She forced herself to walk sedately downstairs to where he was waiting.

Rimada fell upon her with a shriek of joy as they entered the foyer. She paused just long enough for Guake to say hullo too, and then embarked on a monologue which included her future, her new clothes, her reasons for being in London, and lastly Guake's many good points. She only stopped when Adam put a glass into her hand and said: 'Drink up, Rimtsje, our table's ready.'

Over their excellent dinner, he told them about Loveday's encounter that evening, and Guake said gravely: 'A very unnerving experience, Loveday – you shouldn't go out alone in the evening, you know,' and Rimada had echoed him warmly, only the Baron said nothing, which annoyed her very much; presumably she wasn't of sufficient importance to merit his concern, yet he had seemed concerned enough at the time. She went into a brown study and was only reminded of her surroundings when Rimada asked her gaily: 'You will come over, won't you, Loveday? It's to be a big party; Guake has so many friends and so have I, and a betrothal is so exciting.' Her blue eyes shone at the thought of it. 'And of course, there's Adam too, but he will have his party after ours.'

The words dripped like ice cold water into Loveday's head. 'Why is Adam giving a party?' she asked, and achieved a smile as gay as Rimada's own.

Her friend gave her a reproachful look. 'You've not been listening – first our party, then Adam's. His will be huge . . .'

Loveday speared some of the delicious flan on her plate and didn't look up. 'Oh, are you getting married too?' she asked lightly.

His own voice was equally light. 'We all come to it, Loveday. Does it surprise you?'

The flan tasted of nothing; there was a stone somewhere inside her which prevented her from swallowing it. She said carefully: 'No, but Rimmy said that you were a gay bachelor.' She smiled vaguely in his direction and drank some of the excellent claret in her glass.

'So was Guake, and look what's happened to him.' There was a general laugh and Rimada began to babble on again, saving Loveday from the difficulty of making lighthearted conversation when her heart was lead.

The party broke up soon afterwards with Rimada and Guake going back to their hotel and Adam hailing a taxi, putting Loveday in, and then, despite her protests, getting in beside her. As it moved off down the quiet street, he leaned back in his corner, stretched his long legs, and invited her: 'Do tell about your journey to Schiphol. Did you thumb a lift?'

There was no point in keeping it a secret and it would give her something to talk about; anything better than sitting in an awkward silence. He laughed a good deal when she had finished, which she considered rather heartless of him.

'The intrepid Miss Pearce,' he remarked, and no more than that. But at the hospital he got out too and walked through the main doors with her and when she would have wished him good night after a rather prim thank you, caught her hand. 'Not so fast,' he said placidly. 'I'll run you home tomorrow.'

'How did you know that I had days off? And anyway, I'm not free until four o'clock. Who told you?'

He frowned, apparently deep in thought. 'Now I wonder who could have told me?' he sounded vague. 'And four o'clock suits me very well.' He beamed at her with that air of benevolence which she had come to distrust. 'Do you suppose your mother will ask me to stay for supper?'

She remembered the splendid hospitality she had received at his home in Friesland. 'Yes, of course.' She found herself smiling, suddenly happy. 'I'll be ready about half past four – will that do? Where shall I meet you?'

'At the entrance.' He moved a little nearer to her. 'Why were you crying this evening, Loveday?'

She hadn't expected it; she said, her voice a little high: 'I can't remember – it wasn't important.'

'A poor memory for such a very competent young woman. Perhaps you won't remember this either.'

He swooped and caught her close and kissed her in a manner which, she realized shakily, she would remember for ever.

'Oh,' said Loveday, 'good night, Adam,' and fled into the fastness of the Nurses' Home.

There wasn't much of a list the next day – Gordon Blair had a day off; she supposed that one or other of the housemen would be assisting Mr. Gore-Symes. It was a total surprise when, instead of a houseman, Adam walked in with the consulting surgeon.

'Morning, Loveday,' said Mr. Gore-Symes. 'Professor de Wolff hasn't anything to do this morning, so he's giving me a hand. I want to be away myself by half past three, so look sharp, girl.'

She handed towels and swabs and instruments with her usual calm, not looking at Adam after their brief exchange of greetings. It was natural enough, she supposed, since Adam was a good friend of several of the consultants, that he should offer to give a hand; there was some sort of meeting of the senior members of the hospital staff that afternoon, and presumably he would be going. She got on with her work, saying nothing.

The morning list was over by half past eleven, and the two men, with the briefest of thanks, disappeared. Loveday and her nurses cleared the theatre and started to prepare it for the afternoon session – a brief one; an appendix, a couple of hernias and the closing of a colostomy. There was time for once for everyone to have their dinner, time even for a cup of tea in the Sisters' Sitting-Room afterwards. Someone had turned on the electric fire, for it was a chilly, grey day, and they crowded round it, gossiping idly.

'Did I see Professor de Wolff in the corridor this morning?' asked Nancy. 'If I hadn't decided on George, I'd make a dead set at him – he turns me on.'

There was a murmur of assent. 'What a hope,' said someone. 'Did he go to theatre, Loveday?'

'Yes,' said Loveday sedately, while the mere mention

of his name sent her heart pounding. 'Gordon had a day off, you know, so he gave a hand.'

'And what a hand!' sighed Doris White, the Surgical Sister. 'The size of a plate – not that I'd mind . . .'

Everyone laughed. 'He'll have some girl in Holland,' commented Nancy. 'The nice ones always do – or a wife.'

Her words put Loveday in mind of what Rimada had said. She put down her cup and with an excuse that she had to be back in theatre, left the cheerful, laughing little group. Perhaps, she thought uneasily as she went through the hospital, she shouldn't have accepted his offer of a lift, but it was too late to do anything about that now, only she would take care not to go out with him again. Borne along on this high-minded resolution, she reached the theatre.

He was back again that afternoon; he and Mr. Gore-Symes snipped and cut and sewed their way through the list with skilled speed and left together at half past three, wishing her a polite good-bye as they went, and although she had expected Adam to say something about seeing her later, he didn't.

Half an hour later, she was in her own room, fever-ishly going through her wardrobe, deciding finally on the new winter coat she hadn't yet had the opportunity of wearing. It was grey and brown and tawny, cut to show off her neat waist and flaring out around her long legs. She picked a cream woollen dress to wear under it and tucked a tawny scarf into its open collar. It was a splendid opportunity to wear the new shoes and hand-bag she had bought at Raynes, too – bought, she had never quite admitted to herself, in the hope of just such an occasion as this one.

The Baron was standing by the entrance, talking to a group of consultants, who smiled discreetly as Loveday approached and melted back a few yards without appearing to do so, so that Adam was left to walk forward to meet her. She went outside with him, conscious of several pairs of eyes watching them, and got into the Rolls. As Adam got in beside her she said a little shyly: 'I didn't know you had the car with you.'

'A taxi is sometimes quicker, although I don't like them – you see I came on the offchance yesterday evening.'

She digested this in silence. 'Oh – when do you go back?'

She heard his chuckle. 'Speeding me on my way, dear girl? Now, which road do we take?' And when she had told him: 'You look very pretty in that outfit – is that a new coat?'

Her feminine heart reacted at once even while common sense told her that this was no way to start an outing with a man reputed to be on the brink of marrying some other girl. She told him yes briefly and went on to the safe topic of the day's work. But she was allowed to do this for only a short time, for presently he said: 'What a waste of time this is when we have everything else under the sun to talk about.'

'Well, if you don't like my conversation, you do the talking,' said Loveday huffily. Which he did. He talked about his home and Friesland and, briefly, his work; he talked about Rimada and the enormous wedding his aunt would doubtless think necessary. 'I don't care for large weddings, do you?' he wanted to know casually.

'Well, it must be marvellous to wear white satin and orange blossom just once,' Loveday pondered aloud, 'but nice to slip away and get married in some little church – just family, you know.'

They were on the A20, going towards Maidstone at a speed she hardly noticed in the comfort of the big car.

'I have no family.'

'Well, aunts and uncles and cousins, surely? and plenty of friends. I expect you will have a big wedding too.' The very idea made her feel sick.

He considered before he spoke. 'No. A very large party, certainly.' His voice was bland. 'I believe Rimada told you that.'

'Yes, she did. Here's Maidstone, you want the A274 and then at Biddenden you take the A272.'

It was dark now, but inside the car it was cosily warm, a little secure world of their own. She forced her mind away from the wedding he seemed so anxious to talk about and embarked on a dissertation on the surrounding countryside – a complete waste of time, considering it was now too dark to see any of it.

Home looked pleasant as Adam drew to a gentle halt before its door. There were lights in most of the windows, the sound of a dog barking, and Phyllis's voice raised in excitement from somewhere upstairs. Loveday leaned across Adam and blew a few notes on the Rolls' dignified horn, and at once there was a rush of feet and a banging of doors as her family came to the door.

She wondered afterwards what Adam had thought of them all. She had introduced him – her father, quiet and retiring, making him welcome, her mother, instantly won over and asking him to stay to supper almost before they had got into the sitting-room, and Phyllis, tearing downstairs and stopping at their foot to stare. 'Golly,' she exclaimed, 'aren't you super? You turn me on – why, you've got Mick Jagger beaten hollow!'

Loveday had never seen the Baron at a loss, but now, just for a moment, he was; for one thing, she was almost certain that he had no idea who Mick Jagger was, for another, he had been taken by surprise. She said rapidly: 'This is Phyllis, my youngest sister,' and then smiled across at her. 'This is Professor Baron de Wolff van Ozinga.' It sounded impressive.

'Come again,' invited her sister with a charm which robbed her words of rudeness. She twinkled at him pertly. 'I think you're nice, even with a name like that. Are you married?' She had offered him a hand and was grinning up at him.

The members of her family spoke at the same time. 'Your manners, Phyllis!' reminded her father firmly.

'Philly dear,' remonstrated her mother, 'you simply mustn't . . .'

'The Professor's getting married very shortly,' said Loveday in a tight little voice before she could stop herself, and hoped that no one would mention the subject again.

The Baron stood quietly, very relaxed, his eyes

bright under their sleepy lids. He was watching Loveday and when she had spoken, he smiled, a smile which came and went before anyone saw it.

'I'm not sure if I know this Mick Jagger,' he said easily, 'but I suspect a compliment. Thank you, Phyllis.' He gave her a smile which captivated that young lady's heart on the instant.

Supper, a simple meal hastily reinforced with a soup Mrs. Pearce had simmering, and an apple tart which had been destined for the following day, was a cheerful meal with a great deal of talk on everyone's part, although Loveday, while contributing the right answers to any questions asked of her, had little to say for herself. They had finished the tart and were about to drink their coffee in the sitting-room when Mrs Pearce asked: 'Do you have to go back to London this evening? There's plenty of room for you here if you would care to spend the night, and we should all love to have you, Professor – or should I say Baron?'

He laughed. 'Neither. Adam, if you don't mind, Mrs. Pearce. And thank you for your offer, but I'm afraid that I must go back.' He glanced at Loveday, who was trying to look as though she wasn't listening. 'Rimada is with me, as I think I told you.'

'You don't look old enough to be Rimmy's guardian,' remarked the irrepressible Phyllis. 'Is she pretty, the girl you're going to marry?'

He smiled at her. 'She's beautiful,' he said softly.

It was Mr. Pearce who spoke next; he said quite sharply, 'Phyllis, that will do, no more questions.' He addressed himself to his guest. 'A pity that you have to

173

return; perhaps we shall have the pleasure of seeing you again? I have some splendid floribunda roses, still in bloom, which I should like you to see.'

They talked roses and gardens after that until the Baron took himself off, having said almost nothing to Loveday, according her only the briefest of good-byes and making no reference to seeing her again. Naturally, said common sense, since he was to marry some girl in his own country. Loveday, a prey to all the exaggerations of those in love, conjured up a vision of blue eyes and blonde hair in super clothes and with a cold and heartless nature which would reduce the Baron to misery within a year of his wedding. She was only roused from this melancholy reflection by her mother repeating her question several times; it was an unimportant question – she answered it at random, turning such a woebegone face to her parent that that lady began a brisk conversation about the forthcoming church fête, rambling on and on while her daughter recovered herself.

Loveday worked very hard while she was home, helping her father in the garden, tiring herself out, and at the end of her two days' leave went back to hospital, her face grown a little white through sleepless nights, her temper frayed with the effort of putting a good face on a situation which she felt to be hopeless. And although reason told her that she had created the situation for herself anyway, and the Baron had never given any indication that he liked her, let alone loved her – had indeed used her to suit his own purpose, this couldn't alter the fact that her heart was broken.

CHAPTER NINE

A WEEK went by, very slowly, each day beginning with the hope that there would be a letter, a telephone call, even an unexpected appearance of Adam's large person around the next corner of a corridor, or waiting on the other side of a closed door, and ending with no hope at all and another night of staring into the dark until sheer exhaustion closed her eyes. It wasn't until Nancy took her to task for snapping everyone's head off that Loveday pulled herself together, flinging herself into a round of off-duty activities which, while passing the time, did nothing to mend the situation. She had even, in a moment of weakness, allowed herself to be persuaded into going to the cinema with Terry, and then wished she hadn't, for he seemed to think that she was encouraging him, which made it necessary for her to spend the next few days avoiding him. Indeed, it was a puzzle to get over to the Home after duty without encountering him, and she found herself being a little early or late and going a different way through the hospital, and even then she couldn't always avoid him.

On one such evening, ten days or so after her return, meeting him as she left the theatre and hard pressed for an excuse not to accept his offer of dinner that evening, she providentially remembered that she had never gone back to visit the old woman in Summer Street.

She had never intended to go after dark, but rendered reckless by the urgency of supplying a good excuse to Terry, she declared that she was spending the evening with a friend and was in a great hurry to change. Carried along on a wave of bravado and shame at her forgetfulness, she changed, and, her shopping basket over one arm, went first to the row of little shops near the hospital and still conveniently open. Here she purchased tea, sugar, biscuits and a box of chocolates, and repaired without loss of time to Summer Street. She didn't much like it when she turned off the main road and entered its dim dreariness, but she had brought a torch with her this time, a large heavy one, which she intended to use as a weapon of defence should the occasion arise. But no one interfered with her as she walked deliberately along the greasy road. She listened to her footfalls echoing loudly against the blank walls on one side of her, while her heart beat a furious tattoo even more loudly.

The old lady was at home and delighted to see her. 'I knew yer'd come,' she said in a satisfied voice. 'I told the gent yer would, though 'e weren't best pleased at the idea of yer comin' 'ere after dark, I can tell yer.' She led the way into the living-room. 'And if she do, 'e said, I'll trouble yer ter get the neighbour ter walk 'er up the road again.' She nodded her old head. 'And so I shall, Sister, seein' as 'ow 'e's been so good ter me.' She waved a stiff arm. 'Look 'ere.'

Loveday looked, hardly believing her eyes; the little room was still hideous, with its brown paint and dingy wallpaper, but now there was a bright fire burning in the grate and the chairs on either side of it were new, as was the small round table covered by a truly hideous chenille cloth. Her eyes rested on it in stunned disbelief; surely no one would buy anything as awful – green and yellow with a fringe. Her hostess saw her look and said proudly: 'I chose it – 'e took me ter the shop in the 'igh Street and 'e says: Now, me dear, you get just what you like. Nice, ain't it?'

'Lovely,' declared Loveday faintly, and tore her gaze away to stare at the vivid cushions in the chairs, the garish glass lampshade and the bright red rug before the fire. 'Very nice,' she added, feeling that she must say something. 'Who . . . that is, when—?'

'Soon after yer left,' explained her companion, ''e came back the next day – 'ad me address from the 'orspital, 'e said – told me 'e'd 'ad a bit o' luck and 'ad a bit ter spare. Give me an 'ole box of groceries, too.'

Which reminded Loveday of her own purchases. She produced them now and was invited to share a cup of tea and try one of the chocolates while she listened to the old lady's gossip. Presently, when she paused for breath, Loveday asked: 'Did he come back again?'

'Oh, yes – ten days ago. Bin over ter see a friend, 'e 'ad. Brought me one o' them thick shawls, too; said it was fer me birthday, whenever that was.' She laughed richly. 'I 'ain't 'ad a birthday in years!'

Dear kind Adam, thought Loveday. Even if I never see him again, here's a bit more of him to remember. She got up to go presently and the old lady, true to her word, rapped on her wall and when a small, meeklooking man came to the door, she introduced him as

Loveday's escort. He didn't look capable of frightening anyone or anything, but at least he was company; it wasn't until she had bidden her hostess good-bye and they had shut the door behind them that she discovered that he was carrying a serviceable-looking stick and that a large, bad-tempered-looking dog, rejoicing in the unlikely name of Prince, was waiting patiently on the pavement.

When she thanked the little man for his company as they parted and patted the dog's head, her companion shrugged off her gratitude. 'Don't 'ave ter thank me,' he told her forthrightly, ' 'e give me a fiver.'

The information, thus baldly given, of Adam's thoughtfulness warmed her dejected thoughts; somehow he didn't seem so far away as a consequence.

And nor was he. He was in theatre the next morning – an unexpected visit, explained Mr. Gore-Symes with unexpected smoothness; a patient admitted some days ago under his care had taken a turn for the worse and shown such symptoms which, it appeared, might possibly be dealt with by Professor de Wolff's new technique. Loveday heard him out, struck dumb with surprise and delight, while her heart hammered in her throat, choking her. Adam, beyond wishing her good morning, had said nothing; he might have been in his own theatre in Holland, greeting his Theatre Sister on a routine morning. A kind of despair flooded through her damping down the happiness; she turned to the Mayo's table and began, quite unnecessarily, to rearrange the instruments upon it. He had hardly noticed her, his mind was wholly filled with that detestable girl waiting for him in his own country. She scowled so fiercely behind her mask that the nurses looked around them apprehensively, wondering what was wrong.

The morning went well. Perhaps because she was so miserable she was even more efficient than usual, and as for Adam, he worked vigorously, relaxed and friendly but never wasting a word in her direction. The case took a long time; they had their coffee after it and then, after the briefest of halts, went on to the remainder of the list. It was past one o'clock by the time they had finished, and the afternoon list began at half past two. Once the theatre was cleared, an undertaking put into action the moment the surgeons had gone from it, Loveday sent the nurses to their dinner and went along to her office, where the theatre orderly had left a tray of tea and some sandwiches for her. She hadn't wanted a meal; she didn't particularly want the sandwiches, but she supposed that she would have to eat something; the afternoon list would last until four o'clock at least. She poured tea and wondered what she would do with her evening; none of its probable activities interested her; she opened an instrument catalogue and started to leaf through it idly. She was studying a self-retaining catheter, tastefully ringed round with intestinal clamps and a couple of pairs of Judd's basting forceps, all overpoweringly coloured, when the swing doors at the end of the corridor, cutting off the theatre unit from the rest of the hospital, swung open and a moment later her own office door was pushed wide.

'Ah, sandwiches,' said the Baron with satisfaction, and pulled up the only other chair in the room, to sit opposite her across the desk.

Loveday pushed the plate towards him. 'Have you had no lunch?' she asked, and her voice shook a little despite her calm manner.

'No. I wanted to talk to you before I go. Is there enough coffee?'

She opened a drawer in her desk and produced another mug, silently filled it and offered it to him. 'It's tea,' she told him.

He bit deeply into a sandwich and Loveday, watching him and wondering what he was going to say, nibbled hers, glad that she had something to do. When the silence became unbearable she asked in a polite voice: 'I hope Rimada and her mother are well?'

'I want you to come to the party I am giving,' he observed, completely ignoring her remark. 'In three days' time – you see that I have stolen a march on Rimada and Guake.'

She drank some tea; she felt peculiar, as though it was some other girl sitting in her chair and she was watching. She put her mug down carefully. 'I'm so sorry, I shan't be able to – I shall be working.'

'That can be arranged. If I see to things for you, will you come?'

'No.' She took a bite of sandwich and he asked quietly: 'Why not?'

'I shan't know anyone – none of your friends. I can think of no earthly reason why I should come.'

'Shall I give you a very good reason?' He was smiling very disarmingly at her, but she didn't smile back. The only reason she could think of was so that she might meet the blue-eyed blonde who had him in her toils, and wish her happiness and be forced to admire a ring the size of St. Paul's, no doubt. She bit off a scream of pure rage and unhappiness and despair, and without a word, got out of her chair and ran from the little room, down the corridor and into the main hospital. There was still twenty minutes before the afternoon list should start; she would have to find somewhere to hide until then; by that time Adam would be gone and she would never have to see him again.

She burst into tears and shot into the Accident Room to take refuge in Nancy's office. That young lady took one look at her face, fetched tea from the kitchen, added a good splash of brandy from the medicine cupboard and found a box of tissues. 'Don't say a word if you don't want to,' she advised. 'I must get on with the work, Staff's at her dinner and there's that case to admit. Drink your tea, love, and do your face – there's my make-up in my bag, use that. See you later.'

She went away, and Loveday, knowing that her friend's advice was sound, took it, and ten minutes later, looking, save for rather pink eyelids, very much as usual, went back to theatre. Staff and the others were already there, so she went to scrub up. She was adjusting her gloves to a nicety when Mr. Gore-Symes joined her. He had barely turned on the taps when Adam joined him at the next wash basin.

Loveday stopped short, her sterile gloved hands clasped before her sterile green-clad person. 'I thought you were going . . .' she began, betrayed into speech by her surprise.

'Not before we have had our little talk,' he told her over his shoulder. His eyes regarded her steadily above his mask and she had the absurd feeling that he was smiling.

'I'm busy for the rest of the day,' she almost snapped her answer, and made for the door. It was a pity he ignored this; perhaps he hadn't heard. 'I'll be busy,' she repeated, loudly this time.

It was Mr. Gore-Symes who answered her. 'I take it that the patient is ready, Sister?' he queried in his gentle voice, and without a word Loveday went through into theatre to take up her usual position at the patient's foot – it was an abdominal and the anaesthetist and Donald were already there. She gathered her own force around her and stood like a patient statue until the two men arrived. As she handed the towels and towel clips she thought how wonderful it would be if she could drop the lot and run out of the theatre, out of the hospital – miles and miles away; even as she toyed with this preposterous idea she was offering Mr. Gore-Symes his scalpel, the Spencer-Wells forceps, the tissue forceps, some swabs . . .

The list was neither long nor complicated; it was over by four o'clock and all three men went away together. Loveday sent the nurses to tea and waited impatiently for Staff to return, although there was no point in her impatience; she had no plans for the evening and no idea what she would do with it. A nice solitary place in which to cry would be ideal, but she couldn't cry for ever, she would have to pick up the pieces and start again. She gave a watery giggle as she strung the forceps on to their rings; Terry had stopped her that morning and asked her to have dinner with him that evening and once again she had said no; she would change her mind and go after all. It would be awful, but it would get her through an intolerable evening. Surely in the morning, after a night's sleep, she would feel more rational, more able to think clearly.

Her thoughts now were chaotic; a mass of vivid pictures of the Baron engaged, married – living in his lovely house with that horrible girl, whoever she was. Loveday snapped the retractors together viciously as Staff came back, tore off her gown and mask and cap, pinned on the small starched and frilled headdress the sisters of the Royal City were privileged to wear, and with a modicum of words as she handed over the keys, went off duty.

She went circumspectly, longing yet terrified of meeting Adam. He was in the hall as she crossed it, talking to Mr. Gore-Symes, but he had his back to her and couldn't possibly have seen her – if she could get across to the Home – At its door she looked back over her shoulder; he was crossing the courtyard without haste, in her direction. She flew through the door, slammed it shut and ran down the narrow passage to the Sisters' sitting-room.

There were quite a number of Sisters there, sitting round the fire. She skirted round them, oblivious of their surprised glances at her strained white face. She had barely seated herself in the window when there was a tap on the door and the Baron walked in.

A lesser man might have been unnerved at the sight of a dozen girls staring at him, but not Adam. Probably he hadn't noticed them; he had eyes only for Loveday as he closed the door and then stood leaning against it.

'Dear girl,' he declared genially, 'how I do waste my time chasing you around!' He smiled as he spoke; the smile was for her alone, no one else there counted.

'You can't come in here,' she said wildly.

He gave her an innocent stare. 'Why not? There is no notice saying so, and my dearest love, if you insist on receiving my proposal of marriage before a large number of witnesses, then I must allow you your whim.'

She choked, 'Whim? You simply can't – it's not a whim – I never . . .'

His voice was bland. 'Well, I do think it's a better idea if we were to be alone.' He beamed round at the ring of interested faces turned towards him. 'I'm sure all you young ladies will agree – such a personal matter,' he added, still very bland.

They smiled back at him as they got to their feet and filed through the door which he was holding open. When the last one had gone, he closed it once more and leaned his shoulder against it, this time with his hands in his pockets. 'My darling,' he began.

'I'm not your darling!' snapped Loveday, her nerves stretched like violin strings, her voice a little shrill with emotion, lacked conviction.

'Oh, yes, you are.'

But she broke in, almost shouting. 'I'm not – I'm not

– you're going to be married!'

She stared across at him, standing there so calmly. Didn't he feel anything at all? she wondered, while she was bursting with rage and unhappiness and a vicious wish to hurt him.

'So I am,' his deep voice rang out strongly. 'I'm a man who likes the idea of having a wife to love and cherish and children to love too, although I suppose with you, dear heart, I shall have to put up with a certain amount of nagging.'

She gaped at him. 'Nagging? I ... Rimada said ...'

'Rimada says so much. As I have told you before, my little love, she is a nice girl and I am fond of her, but she is sometimes a little stupid.'

'The party?' She wished that Adam would come a little nearer.

'Oh, yes, indeed I am giving a party – a very large one, I should warn you, so that we may celebrate our engagement and you may be introduced to my friends.'

'A large party?' Loveday's powers of conversation had deserted her, she could only repeat what Adam had said. 'Introduce me? Oh, Adam – me?'

'You, dear heart, and no one else. I am astonished that you could imagine that our meeting could end in any other fashion.'

'But we didn't like each other.'

He crossed the room at last and took her in his arms. 'Did I ever say that?' he wanted to know. 'What would you have done if, the moment I had clapped eyes on you, I had caught you and kissed you – like this?' He kissed her until her head swam. 'And then asked you to marry me. I'm asking you now, my darling – it has been on the tip of my tongue a thousand times, but I wanted you to be sure.'

She said, her voice a little muffled by his shoulder: 'You called me a meddlesome busybody.'

'And so you were, although a delightful one. Were you a bossy little girl?'

She chuckled into his jacket. 'I don't know – probably.'

He kissed the top of her head with pleasure. 'Ah, well, I suppose in due time we shall have some bossy little daughters.'

She looked up at him then. 'Oh, Adam – but there must be a little boy too, so he can be a surgeon when he grows up.'

'But of course.' He smiled down at her tenderly. 'How well we agree.' He looked about him, still holding her tightly. 'My dearest darling, I do not care for this room; we will go somewhere else, somewhere pleasant where we can make plans.'

'You mean to tell me,' asked Loveday, quite astonished, 'that you haven't made any plans? But you're always making them and then everyone does what you want them to do.'

He held her back against his arm so that he could look into her, and she gazed back at him. He looked most satisfyingly in love with her, he also looked smug; she had seen that look before.

'Plans?' his voice was smoothly content. 'Well, I may

have thought up one or two ideas, my darling. It seemed sensible to get together all the necessary papers for our marriage – I happen to have them in my pocket – and there's the small matter of you leaving this place at a moment's notice.'

'You thought that up too?'

'Oh, yes, I had that settled some days ago.' He added with an air of innocence: 'I would have told you sooner, my pretty, but I was a little uncertain about sweeping you off your feet.'

Her mouth curved into a smile that was all love and delight.

'Adam darling, you've never been uncertain about anything in your life, have you?' She wreathed her arms round his neck and kissed him. 'Besides, I'd love – just once – to be swept off my feet.'

She kissed him again for good measure.

Why the smile?

... because she has just received her **Free Harlequin Romance Catalogue!**

... and now she has a complete listing of the many, many Harlequin Romances still available.

... and now she can pick out titles by her favorite authors or fill in missing numbers for her library.

You too may have a **Free Harlequin Romance Catalogue** (and a smile!), simply by writing to:

HARLEQUIN READER SERVICE

DEPARTMENT C
M.P.O. BOX 707
NIAGARA FALLS N.Y.
14302

Canadian Address:
STRATFORD, ONTARIO
CANADA

Be sure to include your name and address!

Please Note: Harlequin Romance Catalogue of available titles is revised every three months.

BY POPULAR DEMAND

4 *Harlequin Presents...*

EVERY MONTH

OVER THE YEARS many favourite Harlequin Romance authors have written novels which have not been available to Harlequin Romance. Now, because of the overwhelming response to Harlequin Presents, they are allowing us to publish these original works in the Harlequin Presents series. Authors such as Roberta Leigh, Rachel Lindsay, Rosalind Brett and Margaret Rome will be joining Anne Hampson, Anne Mather and Violet Winspear enabling us to publish 4 titles per month on a continuing basis.

Look for these books at your local bookseller, or use the handy order coupon. See title listing on following page.

PLEASE NOTE: All Harlequin Presents novels from #83 onwards are 95c. Books below that number, **where available** are priced at 75c through Harlequin Reader Service until December 31st, 1975.

Harlequin Presents..

Some of the world's greatest romance authors.

ROSALIND BRETT
- [ ] #55 LOVE THIS STRANGER
- [ ] #71 AND NO REGRETS

MARY BURCHELL
- [ ] #67 ACCOMPANIED BY HIS WIFE
- [ ] #75 DARE I BE HAPPY?

ANNE HAMPSON
- [ ] #16 WINGS OF NIGHT
- [ ] #19 SOUTH OF MANDRAKI
- [ ] #31 BLUE HILLS OF SINTRA
- [ ] #34 STORMY THE WAY
- [ ] #37 AN EAGLE SWOOPED
- [ ] #40 WIFE FOR A PENNY
- [ ] #47 WHEN THE CLOUDS PART
- [ ] #51 HUNTER OF THE EAST
- [ ] #56 AFTER SUNDOWN
- [ ] #59 BELOVED RAKE
- [ ] #63 STARS OVER SARAWAK
- [ ] #72 THE WAY OF A TYRANT
- [ ] #79 THE BLACK EAGLE

MARGERY HILTON
- [ ] #52 A MAN WITHOUT MERCY

ROBERTA LEIGH
- [ ] #64 BELOVED BALLERINA
- [ ] #68 AND THEN CAME LOVE
- [ ] #76 HEART OF THE LION

RACHEL LINDSAY
- [ ] #48 BUSINESS AFFAIR
- [ ] #53 MASK OF GOLD
- [ ] #60 CASTLE IN THE TREES
- [ ] #73 FOOD FOR LOVE
- [ ] #80 INNOCENT DECEPTION

ANNE MATHER
- [ ] # 8 THE SANCHEZ TRADITION
- [ ] #11 WHO RIDES THE TIGER
- [ ] #14 STORM IN A RAIN BARREL
- [ ] #17 LIVING WITH ADAM
- [ ] #20 A DISTANT SOUND OF THUNDER
- [ ] #32 JAKE HOWARD'S WIFE
- [ ] #35 SEEN BY CANDLELIGHT
- [ ] #38 MOON WITCH
- [ ] #46 PRELUDE TO ENCHANTMENT
- [ ] #49 A SAVAGE BEAUTY
- [ ] #54 THE NIGHT OF THE BULLS
- [ ] #57 LEGACY OF THE PAST
- [ ] #61 CHASE A GREEN SHADOW
- [ ] #65 WHITE ROSE OF WINTER
- [ ] #69 MASTER OF FALCON'S HEAD
- [ ] #74 LEOPARD IN THE SNOW
- [ ] #77 THE JAPANESE SCREEN

KARIN MUTCH
- [ ] #66 CINDY, TREAD LIGHTLY

MARGARET ROME
- [ ] #58 MAN OF FIRE
- [ ] #62 THE MARRIAGE OF CAROLINE LINDSAY

KAY THORPE
- [ ] #81 THE IRON MAN

MARGARET WAY
- [ ] #78 A MAN LIKE DAINTREE
- [ ] #82 COPPER MOON

VIOLET WINSPEAR
- [ ] # 9 WIFE WITHOUT KISSES
- [ ] #12 DRAGON BAY
- [ ] #15 THE LITTLE NOBODY
- [ ] #21 THE UNWILLING BRIDE
- [ ] #30 BRIDE OF LUCIFER
- [ ] #33 FORBIDDEN RAPTURE
- [ ] #36 LOVE'S PRISONER
- [ ] #39 TAWNY SANDS
- [ ] #50 THE GLASS CASTLE
- [ ] #70 THE CHATEAU OF ST. AVRELL

ALL BOOKS LISTED 75c

These titles are available at your local bookseller, or through
the Harlequin Reader Service, M.P.O. Box 707, Niagara Falls,
N.Y. 14302; Canadian address 649 Ontario St., Stratford, Ont.

E

Have You Missed Any of These

Harlequin Romances?

☐ 1051 BRIDE OF ALAINE
Rose Burghley

☐ 1052 MEANT FOR EACH OTHER
Mary Burchell

☐ 1074 NEW SURGEON AT ST.
LUCIAN'S, Elizabeth
Houghton

☐ 1076 BELLS IN THE WIND
Kate Starr

☐ 1087 A HOME FOR JOCELYN
Eleanor Farnes

☐ 1094 MY DARK RAPPAREE
Renrietta Reid

☐ 1098 THE UNCHARTED OCEAN
Margaret Malcolm

☐ 1102 A QUALITY OF MAGIC
Rose Burghely

☐ 1103 HEART OF GOLD
Marjorie Moore

☐ 1106 WELCOME TO PARADISE
Jill Tahourdin

☐ 1115 THE ROMANTIC HEART
Norrey Ford

☐ 1118 LAMENT FOR LOVE
Jean S. Macleod

☐ 1120 HEART IN HAND
Margaret Malcolm

☐ 1121 TEAM DOCTOR, Ann Gilmour

☐ 1122 WHISTLE AND I'LL COME
Flora Kidd

☐ 1124 THE NEW ZEALANDER
Joyce Dingwall

☐ 1138 LOVING IS GIVING
Mary Burchell

☐ 1144 THE TRUANT BRIDE
Sara Seale

☐ 1150 THE BRIDE OF MINGALAY
Jean S. Macleod

☐ 1166 DOLAN OF SUGAR HILLS
Kate Starr

☐ 1167 DEAR BARBARIAN
Janice Gray

☐ 1170 RED LOTUS
Catherine Airlie

☐ 1172 LET LOVE ABIDE
Norrey Ford

☐ 1180 ROSE OF THE DESERT
Roumelia Lane

☐ 1182 GOLDEN APPLE ISLAND
Jane Arbor

PLEASE NOTE: All Harlequin Romances from #1857 onwards are 75c. Books below that number, **where available** are priced at 60c through Harlequin Reader Service until December 31st, 1975.

Have You Missed Any of These Harlequin Romances?

☐ 446 TO PLEASE THE DOCTOR
    Marjorie Moore
☐ 458 NEXT PATIENT, DOCTOR
    ANNE, Elizabeth Gilzean
☐ 468 SURGEON OF DISTINCTION
    Mary Burchell
☐ 486 NURSE CARIL'S NEW POST
    Caroline Trench
☐ 487 THE HAPPY ENTERPRISE
    Eleanor Farnes
☐ 503 NURSE IN CHARGE
    Elizabeth Gilzean
☐ 555 LOVE THE PHYSICIAN
    Hilda Nickson
☐ 584 VILLAGE HOSPITAL
    Margaret Malcolm
☐ 683 DESIRE FOR THE STAR
    Averil Ives
    (Original Harlequin title
    "Doctor's Desire")
☐ 699 THE HOUSE ON BRINDEN
    WATER   Nan Asquith
    (Original Harlequin title
    "The Doctor Is Engaged")
☐ 701 DOCTOR'S LOVE   Jane Arbor
☐ 744 VERENA FAYRE, PROBA-
    TIONER, Valerie K. Nelson
☐ 745 TENDER NURSE, Hilda Nickson
☐ 746 LOYAL IN ALL, Mary Burchell
    (Original Harlequin title
    "Nurse Marika, Loyal In
    All")
☐ 748 THE VALLEY OF PALMS
    Jean S. Macleod
☐ 757 THE PALM-THATCHED
    HOSPITAL, Juliet Shore
☐ 764 NURSE ANN WOOD
    Valerie K. Nelson
☐ 771 NURSE PRUE IN CEYLON
    Gladys Fullbrook
☐ 772 CHLOE WILDE, STUDENT
    NURSE, Joan Turner
☐ 787 THE TWO FACES OF NURSE
    ROBERTS   Nora Sanderson
☐ 790 SOUTH TO THE SUN
    Betty Beaty
☐ 794 SURGEON'S RETURN
    Hilda Nickson
☐ 812 FACTORY NURSE   Hilary Neal

☐ 825 MAKE UP YOUR MIND NURSE
    Phyllis Matthewman
☐ 841 TRUANT HEART
    Patricia Fenwick
    (Original Harlequin title
    "Doctor in Brazil")
☐ 844 MEET ME AGAIN
    Mary Burchell
    (Original Harlequin title
    "Nurse Alison's Trust")
☐ 850 THE OTHER ANNE
    Caroline Trench
    (Original Harlequin title
    "Nurse Anne's
    Impersonation")
☐ 858 MY SURGEON NEIGHBOUR
    Jane Arbor
☐ 873 NURSE JULIE OF WARD
    THREE   Joan Callender
☐ 878 THIS KIND OF LOVE
    Kathryn Blair
☐ 890 TWO SISTERS
    Valerie K. Nelson
☐ 897 NURSE HILARY'S HOLIDAY
    TASK, Jan Haye
☐ 898 MY DREAM IS YOURS
    Nan Asquith
    (Original Harlequin title
    "Doctor Robert Comes
    Around")
☐ 900 THERE CAME A SURGEON
    Hilda Pressley
☐ 902 MOUNTAIN OF DREAMS
    Barbara Rowan
☐ 903 SO LOVED AND SO FAR
    Elizabeth Hoy
☐ 909 DESERT DOORWAY
    Pamela Kent
☐ 911 RETURN OF SIMON
    Celine Conway
☐ 912 THE DREAM AND THE
    DANCER, Eleanor Farnes
☐ 919 DEAR INTRUDER
    Jane Arbor
☐ 934 MY DEAR COUSIN
    Celine Conway
☐ 936 TIGER HALL
    Esther Wyndham

PLEASE NOTE: All Harlequin Romances from #1857 onwards are 75c. Books below that number, **where available** are priced at 60c through Harlequin Reader Service until December 31st, 1975.